THE ARCHBISHOP
OF APPALACHIA

Stories and Musings from the Archdiocese

JOSEPH F. EDWARDS

JOSEPH F. EDWARDS

Printed Worldwide
First Printing 2025
First Edition 2025

10 9 8 7 6 5 4 3 2 1

ISBN: 978-0-9836530-5-9

Published by Cara Press

Interior Book Design by Walt's Book Design
www.waltsbookdesign.com

Contact: permissions@carapress.com

THE ARCHBISHOP
OF APPALACHIA

Contents

Foreword

I have a theory that all good fiction must be true. I'll leave it to you to unpack that.

Some of these stories and musings have appeared elsewhere with various narrators, including me. If you read all of them, I believe that you will be able to identify one or more threads that give the collection internal cohesion. Is this possibly a novel? I am not going to make that claim, but I am not going to dispute someone who may insist that it is a novel. I am satisfied to state simply that this book is what it is, including its use of different narrators, disparate settings, and an extensive time frame. If you feel like you are getting to know some of these characters as you read the book, I have met my objective.

Joe

The Archbishop Reflects on the Real Archdiocese

These are old mountains. See how round and soft and smooth they are? Oh, it's true that a few of them are jagged and raw, but those are the exception. There is a spirit in these mountains that has matured over the ages through pain and suffering and joy and anticipation and hope. There is a brutal sweetness here that flows from ancient sources, a sweetness that for ages has attracted troubled, searching souls who sometimes through those ages have found their peace, their life, their Jesus. Round, and soft and smooth — a place where a man, or a woman, or a man and a woman, can make a home.

These are old mountains, where one can, and should, live by the seasons. Plant and tend the crop in this season and one will have food to eat in the next season. Here, the crop grows better to the sound of the dulcimer and the fiddle and the banjo. These old mountains proclaim that as truth. But they also proclaim that one should not, cannot, live by bread alone. And here, perhaps more than anywhere, one can find that elusive nourishment that sustains and protects Homo in his inevitable journey through the valley of the shadow of death.

Here reconciliation of the brutal sweetness of independence with the slavery of economic advancement is impossible. They cannot be reconciled. Perhaps some form of détente, or compromise, is possible. Time will tell. But until it dies, which will not happen, the human spirit will demand, and have, something greater than the illusory security of material wealth. Here the painters and the poets and the prophets celebrate that spirit; in the desolate regions they bemoan its loss. In the rich country many of them mock this spirit and celebrate its loss; but they spit against the wind, and their sputum flies back into their faces and soils them and slimes them. And yet even then, there are some in the rich country in whom the spark survives who do bemoan the loss of that spirit; they go into the metropolitan mine shafts that we call the subways, and they paint their pictures there, and the poets and the prophets write their moans and their groans there on the subway walls as they long for eternity. And the Holy Spirit of God hears those moans and groans and translates them and presents them to the Unnamable: Abba, Abba, save us! And Abba says Come to me, and most do not heed that call.

But there are those who do. They flee the cesspools and come to bathe and swim in crystal waters where life abounds. Their neighborhood is a thousand miles from top to bottom. But as time passes they come to see that their hood is not measured in units of distance. Their hood is the community of the free, the society of sapiens. They have escaped the prison of materiality and have come to a realm where they can have peace and rest. That is the real Appalachia. That is the real archdiocese that you will encounter here. It is not an archdiocese where life is always pretty, and easy, and without trouble, but it is a place where glitter is not glory in the view of most who live and die here, and that sets it apart from most of this land.

GAVIN AND MARIA, SCOTLAND 1351 A.D.

A LOOK BACK AT OUR ROOTS

He gagged. The fog stank, and sat heavy on the town. Bodies lay in the street, some freshly dead, some long dead and putrid; and here and there a body trembled slightly, not quite gone. The few who were afoot avoided each other. An occasional dog meandered among the corpses, sniffing as it went.

He must leave this rot. His woman and his son were gone. He felt fortunate that he had been able to get them buried before the gravediggers died. There were three of them counting the one she had carried in her womb for eight months. It remained there, inchoate, when they put her in the ground. All three now lay together. He had yelled at those who had dumped them in. He had expected some dignity in the interment but there was no dignity. The monks shoveled mud and dirt over them as he yelled. They did not look at him. One said, —Friend, you should not complain. Yours at least have their own hole. We put seventeen in one hole this morning before we came here. I doubt any of them knew each other. They came to their hole on the death wagon.

There was nothing but death in this stinking, heavy, immobile fog that shrouded the town. Now the gravediggers were dead, and no one would touch a corpse so they all lay rotting where they had drawn their last breath, in the streets, in the dank interiors, even in the public waters. When he left he would leave nothing because there was nothing. He had the clothes he wore and a sack with a few small loaves in it and a pouch of salt and a cloak and a thick wool blanket and two empty water flasks that he had used in his ventures in the East. He had a blade and an oak staff and a longbow with five dozen arrows in his quiver, and a purse fat and heavy with his own coin. In his youth he had traveled to the Eastern Empire with his master, a noble who had insisted that he learn the skills of a scribe and an archer while he was still a boy. His master had survived in the East, mostly as an administrator, and had returned to the kingdom and had freed his servants, and as he lay dying from this stinking pestilence he summoned his former servants and gave each a leather purse full of silver and gold coin.

There was nothing left in this town but dead and dying bodies, the filth of human detritus, and a stench that filled every space. He must leave today, now. He had been thirsty but the smells had made him gag and had lessened his thirst; there was no beer, no wine, no mead, and the swill in the public fountains was undrinkable. Every day until the last of the friars died they pulled bodies from these fountains. He was thirsty but he had no choice but to wait until he could drink from a spring in the hills, a spring above the towns and away from the hillside villages. He had learned from the Eastern priests that there was bad water and there was good water, and he knew without doubt that there was no good water here; he would find good water, but it would not be here. He would eat his crumbs in time, and he would eat grubs and roots and whatever nature might provide. But he would live. He would leave this town now, and he would live. His choices were to live in the forest or die in the town. He would go to the forest. He knew the forest and he knew that he could live there. There is life in the forest, notwithstanding its mystery and the fear of it because of the occasional wolf or bear, or dark spirit according to some. But he knew where the dark spirit was this day, and he would leave that this morning, right now.

So he left, walking quickly, occasionally looking back to see if there were others behind him. There were none, and by noon he had passed through the city gate. He stopped and looked back for a moment, said goodbye to the dead, and chose his course.

By late afternoon he began to look earnestly for a brook which would indicate a source of good water. Now he was truly thirsty and he needed water. By his reckoning he had traveled ten to twelve miles. He had passed through or skirted several hamlets, and he aimed for a forest that he could see vaguely through the mist three or four miles distant where he could prepare a camp to give him comfort through the night. But his thirst was such that he decided to look for water now, before he got to the forest, where he might not find water before nightfall and surely would not find it in the dark of the night.

He came upon a thin line of vegetation cutting through a field, probably growth sustained by the waters of a tiny stream, he thought. He left the road and cut through the field and came to a brook. Though he was intensely thirsty, he determined to drink from the source of this brook where the water would be clean, and good, and where he could fill his flasks with water to get him through another day of flight from the filth and wretchedness that he had left a few hours back. As he walked upstream he could see a knob of woods ahead on a slope, and beyond that there was no line of vegetation cutting through the field beyond the knob. So the spring would be in that little patch of woods.

Suddenly he stopped. He smelled smoke and it was the smoke of a campfire. The knob was about a quarter of a mile away. Because of the fog, he could not see the smoke, but he knew this smell. This was not the smell of peat burning on a peasant's hearth but of deadwood and some juniper. This would be a campfire. Now, instead of following the brook straight to the trees, he swung out and flanked through the field to approach the knob and the spring from a vantage point above the spring. He took his longbow from his back and nocked an arrow. He stooped as he flanked the little wood and began slowly approaching it from above. When he came to the edge of the growth and entered he saw a woman seated on a fallen log next to a small fire with a toddler beside her. He could hear the gurgle of the spring nearby. He approached, slowly.

—Are you alone?

She did not look up. —I heard you and saw you coming when you flanked us. I have this child. I have goats, three does and a buck. I have a few coins in a pouch. I have God. And now you are here. I am not alone.

—You saw me?

Yes. It is easier to see out from here within this wood than to see in from out there.

—Where are the goats?

—They are browsing somewhere here in the wood. They will come when they come, or when I leave.

—You have no food?

—The child and I have milk from the goats. I know how to pick mushrooms. I know how to catch small animals and fish. The ferns are tasty. I can dig for grubs with my blade; the ground here is full of them and they roast very nicely and taste good. I have a fire steel and flint. I have air in my lungs to start the tinder, unlike most in the city which I left. We have not starved, nor will we, by the grace of God. Where are you going?

—I don't know. I am just going. And you?

She looked at the child, and then into her fire.

—Nor do I know where I am going, Sir. What I do know is that right now I am here by this fire. It feels good.

—Where is your man?

—He is in the city. He will never leave the city.

—He is very foolish.

—He is very dead.

He looked away for a moment.

—Forgive me.

—Done. They buried him a month ago. He has much company there. More than half the city. And most of the rest will soon be dead.

—Yes. But they will not be buried. The gravediggers are dead.

She motioned with a nod, —Sit. I will give you some cheese. I am Maria.

—I am Gavin. Some call me Shanke — the long-legged one.

He drank from the spring and filled his flasks and then took a loaf of bread from his sack and broke it and handed a chunk to her. She broke off a morsel and gave it to the child. They ate.

—What is the child's name?

—I do not know.

He stopped chewing, puzzled, and looked quickly at her and the child. —The child must be two or three years old. Surely you have not waited this long to name it?

—When I left the city I found the child sitting by its dead mother just outside the gate. She had been dead for some time. I watched others walk by without giving the child any attention. I could not do that. I do not condemn the others, but I could not do that.

—How about its father?

—I do not know. I asked the few who were nearby. None knew. Some said the child had been there by its dead mother for two days. I picked him up and put him on my shoulders and left the city with my goats. That was three days ago. He is not heavy, as you can see.

—It is a boy?

—Yes.

He handed the little one a piece of his bread.

She watched them. The light had begun to fade.

—You may camp here tonight if you wish, she said, looking into the fire. It will soon be dark.

He studied the tiny flames. He could think of no compelling reason to proceed to the forest and set up another camp, when there was already comfort here. It was true that he would be three or four miles farther along if he went on to the forest now, but farther along to where? There was plenty of brush and bough here to make a small shelter for himself, as she had already done for herself and the child.

—You are very gracious. I will stay here tonight. I will not violate you.

—Nor I you, she said.

~ ~ ~

When morning came the fog was gone and the goats were back. Two lay near Maria and two near Gavin.

—Would you and yours come with me? he asked Maria, as he began to gather his kit. The goats were already sniffing him and rubbing against him, enjoying their morning. Maria was picking dead black coals from what had been the fire and putting them in a small leather pouch where she kept her flint and steel.

—It would slow you down. The goats do not travel fast, nor does this little one.

He nodded. —True, but that would not matter, would it? We're just going — no destination except to put distance between ourselves and that deadly pestilence, wherever that may be. And it will be safer for us to be together.

He motioned toward the child. —It will surely be better for the little one. We can take turns with him, and there is no need for us to travel fast. We must only keep moving. And the goats will give us food as we go. God brought us together did He not? Or would you prefer to say it was my thirst?

She looked down and smiled. She liked this man. She picked another handful of dead embers one by one and put them in her tinder pouch.

—We will go together.

And so they did. It has been a long journey, too long to recount here in full.

THE SOUP LADY, SOUTHERN APPALACHIA 1847 A.D.

MATERIA MEDICA

There was a mountain woman in the southern Appalachian hills they called the soup lady. She could make soup out of anything, they said. Some of the old-timers said she could make soup out of an old piece of barn wood. In fact, she could.

One day one of her neighbors who lived on the next mountain over came by with his sick wife and asked if there was some kind of soup that might help cure her of whatever it was that was ailing her. The sick woman had a fever and a headache, and a serious case of the shakes and a sore throat.

The old man pulled up on his mule wagon.

—Howdy. Th'old lady's got to hackin' again and she's got the shakes real bad and her throat's ahurtin'er. I'uz wondering if you could cook'er up sump'n that'd help'er?

—Howdy, Lester. I'm shore sorry to hear that. We'll see what we can do. Let's ease her down off that wagon and get her in the house. Hey darlin', we gonna try to get you to feelin' better.

The old man climbed down and helped his woman as she eased down from the wagon, and he and the soup lady helped her onto the porch and into the house.

—You go on back and take care of yore place and we'll take care of what's goin' on here. I'll set up with her if I need to. I'd say come back in about three days. She walked the woman over to a straightbacked chair and helped her sit.

—I shore appreciate it. The man left and the soup lady went back inside and helped the sick woman onto a cot near the fireplace.

—You need a pot before I go out?

The woman shook her head. —I don't think so. I had the runs yesterday, but I ain't had'em this morning.

—Awright, I'll be right back. We're gonna cook you up some medicine. I'm gonna set this chamber pot rightchere just in case.

She went out back to her shed and found a couple of old leftover boards that she had tossed into a corner when she had patched her corn crib a few months back. The wood from which these boards were sawed was heart pine. With a sharp blade the soup lady scraped a couple of the planks and smelled the spot where she had scraped. She picked one and went back in the house and started shaving wood from the plank in paper thin curls. She took a double handful of these shavings and put them in an iron kettle and covered them with water and set the kettle on the fire to boil.

The soup lady then went out to a willow tree that was growing at the edge of her place and with her blade she carefully sliced some bark from a stout branch, making sure that she got the inner bark, and took that back to the fire where the heart pine shavings were simmering. She would wait to put the willow bark in the simmering liquid near the end. She didn't want to kill the good of the bark by heating it too much. The old Cherokee women had taught her that. The sick woman lay on the cot staring blankly and shaking from time to time as the soup lady worked.

After a few minutes the soup lady fed her fire and tossed in the willow bark and stirred the liquid. She would let this simmer and then cool just enough so that the alcohol would not cook off when she poured the warm turpentine and willow broth into the whiskey.

The whole process took about an hour. Once she had her potion mixed up properly it should work quickly. The sick lady should be feeling better long before her husband got back to their place on the next mountain over.

The soup lady had enough potion now to last a few days thanks to a generous measure of whiskey in the mixture. She poured some of the potion into a clay mug, almost filling it, and took this to the sick woman and eased her up into a sitting position. She wanted her to take a heavy dose of this medicine on the first go round. She could sip it later, but she needed to chug it now.

—I want you to take all this right down. Take as big o' swallows as you can.

The woman drank the warm liquid in three or four swallows and exhaled deeply.

—That's good, Sweetie. Let's get you back down now and you rest. I'll put you a pot rightchere. And here's you some fresh spring water to drink. You just keep drinkin' on that. If you feel like you need to go to the outhouse you let me know. We're gonna whup this thing.

Three days later the old man came to fetch his wife. She was up walking around tending a kettle of greens cooking on the fire. She looked good. They all three ate dinner which consisted of greens and cornbread and side meat and clabber. When they had finished the old man helped his wife up onto the mule wagon.

—How much I owe ya?

—Nothin'. It's been a real pleasure havin' her here with me. Just bring me a jug the next time you run off a batch.

—I'll do it.

He done it.

EARL AND JESSIE, CARPE DIEM

APPALACHIA 1851 A.D.

Earl Jackson sat on his porch every evening about thirty minutes before sundown and listened. Earl loved to listen. No matter what time of year he listened he could hear distinct sounds of birds and other critters of the mountain that most would not hear if they did not listen for the sounds they made. And he could hear the trickle of the little brook beside his cabin, and the cackle and cluck of his chickens and the gentle grunting and squealing of his pigs. And all these sounds pleased him, but he went to his porch every evening not to hear just these sounds but also to listen intently to another sound that pricked his heart like good mountain whiskey.

Sometimes it felt good, sometimes it hurt, but always it was worth it.

Another mountain rose on the other side of the little valley down toward which the brook by his place flowed, and on that other mountain Jessie Pender went to her front porch every evening about thirty minutes before sunset and began strumming her old dulcimer and singing to the critters of the mountain, the birds and the rabbits and the squirrels and the gobblers and her pigs and chickens and milk cow. Sometimes Earl thought *Maybe she's singing to me and playing for me too*. Her husband had been gone for almost fifteen years now and she had started going to her porch and playing her dulcimer right after he left. She could see the road from there in several different places as it snaked up the mountain toward her house and then on up to where it crossed the ridge above her place and descended into the next valley toward the town by the river in the bottom of that valley. She looked to see if he might be walking up the road on her mountain, and she looked up to see if he might be coming down the mountain on the road as it descended from the ridge above. She had done this for almost fifteen years now, and from that first day she had brought her dulcimer to the porch and strummed it as she sang and called to her husband, and he never came walking up the road from the valley below or walking down from the ridge above.

Earl listened, and it seemed to him that of an evening when Jessie started singing, a spirit flowed out from her porch and settled over the valley, and then the birds stopped singing and chirping and the pigs stopped squealing, and the other mountain critters stopped and listened and surely were touched by her sounds and by this spirit, as he was. This year the ritual was especially intense because of a dove that flew in and alighted on his split rail fence every evening just as Jessie began strumming and singing. Doves keep one mate, and this for life, and where one goes the other follows. As you travel these mountains watch for that and you will see. But this dove always came alone. It came when Jessie started singing, and it left when she stood and went back inside with her dulcimer. Soon Earl came to believe that this daily appearance of the lone dove was a sign, but he could not fathom what it was signing.

One evening Earl sat on his porch and watched Jessie come out with her dulcimer and start playing. He looked over to the rail fence to watch the dove fly in and alight there. This evening the dove did not come. Earl focused on the absence of the dove more than on Jessie this evening. When the sun had set, Jessie went back inside her house and the dove still did not come. Earl did not sleep well that night.

The next afternoon the same thing happened, and then the following afternoon and the one following that. Earl decided he must go tell Jessie about the dove.

The next day, early in the morning, Earl made the one hour journey by foot to Jessie's house. She saw him coming way down the road and went out to meet him as he neared the path that led up from the road to her front porch.

—What in the world brings you all the way across the draw Earl? You ain't been over here in two or three years.

—Jessie, I got to tell you something that's been happening. I been listening to you play of an evening for quite a while now, and this year a lone dove started flying in and perching on my fence right when you started playing. Then he'd leave when you finished and went back in the house. Trouble is, he ain't showed up this whole week and this is already Friday. It's a sign, Jessie. I'm telling ya I know it in my heart.

They walked up the path to the porch and sat. They looked out across the valley where Earl's house and his outbuildings sat in a patch of green halfway up the other mountain. It wasn't a half a mile away as the crow flies, but it was close to an hour by the road on foot or in a mule wagon.

—He ain't coming back Jessie. I know in my heart it's a sign. He ain't coming back. I know you've been wantin' him to come back for fifteen years now, but he ain't coming Jessie. He's dead. That's got to be what the sign means.

Jessie looked Earl in the eye while he spoke. When he had finished she got up and went inside and after a minute she came back out with her dulcimer. She sat and played slow, and tears splashed from her cheeks onto the instrument in her lap. She played and finally she stopped and looked out across the valley.

This time she did not look down the road into the valley, as she had done for fifteen years, and she did not look up the road toward the ridge above. Earl kept a few sheep, and she looked across the draw at his little flock, which appeared as a tiny white patch against the green pasture. For several minutes she watched the white patch move slowly across the green field. Earl waited and watched her.

—Earl, I know you've been coming out and settin' on your porch watching me just about every day since your sweet Glenda died. I can see ya across the valley there, just like you can see me. That's been seven years Earl. That means little Josh is already seven years old. How's he doin'?

—He's good Jessie. He's a little too skinny. We ain't had a decent home cooked meal since he was born and she died. I've fed him, but I ain't much of a cook, and it's been just him and me. He goes around the hill to his grandma's some, but she stays likkered up. That's where he is right now.

She looked at him, and then looked back across the valley. —Yont me to come cook you some dinner?

Earl was surprised. —I'd love that, Jessie. You talkin' about today noon?

—Yeah, I reckon I am. It ain't even the middle of the mornin' yet. You got a chicken we can dress and fry up? Or maybe make some chicken and pastry?

—I got a yard full o' chickens, and it don't matter how you cook it. You need to get ready or anything?

—Naw not really, but you'll need to go catch the cow and put a lead rope on her. She won't just follow us the whole way over there without a rope on her.

Earl was caught off guard. Normally guests did not bring their cows with them to dinner, even here in these mountains.

—Why in the world would the cow be coming with us Jessie?

She looked back across the draw at the green field with the little white patch moving slowly across it. She looked for a long moment.

—Earl, if I come cook you and Josh some dinner I ain't leavin'. I ain't leavin' tonight, I ain't leavin' tomorrow, I ain't never leavin' Earl, and you know as well as I do that cow's gotta be milked mornin' and evenin' or she'll get the fire in her tits and die on us. I cain't leave her here if I ain't comin' back cause she cain't skip a milkin'. You can come back with a wagon tomorrow and get the pigs and the chickens and whatever else needs to be took care of right away, but if I go I ain't leavin'. You sure you still hungry enough to have me come over and cook you some dinner?

As she spoke, Earl watched her with his mouth hanging open. This had come out of the blue and he was stunned. Earl was generally a slow going, steady man, but this was moving fast.

—I'm about as hungry as a man can get, Jessie.

—Awright. You go catch the cow and I'll pack a sack. You understand dontcha Earl? I ain't never leavin' if I come with ya. You need to get ahold o' that 'fore I come over there.

Earl stood for another moment with his mouth hanging open, staring at her.

—I believe I got that Jessie. I shore do. I'll be back up here with the cow in just a minute. You go ahead and get yore stuff together and we'll go have us some dinner, you and me. Lord have mercy! I reckon I'm fixin' to get me another cow!

And thus it was that Earl and Jessie became Earl and Jessie, and Jessie never left. She never, ever left.

There is a patch of ground in the east of the North American continent that lies roughly between southern New York and the northern reaches of Mississippi, Alabama, and Georgia, where more than twenty-five million people live and procreate. The distance from top to bottom is about one thousand miles as the crow flies. The region includes four hundred and twenty counties in thirteen states, but these twenty-five million people don't pay much attention to counties, states, and other forms of government. They are mostly concerned with eating and drinking, procreation, and doing the will of the Lord. Almost all of their pursuits are conducted within these basic categories of human activity.

These are mostly mountain people. They inhabit both the little mountains of the north and the south and the periphery, and the big, rugged, backbone mountains of the high wild country.

Somehow the character of the people seems to mirror the character of the mountains they inhabit, except that one would be hard put to find more than just a few wild people in the middle country of the big, hard, backbone mountains, probably not more than would reside in any specific aggregation of homo sapiens anywhere. This might be somewhat puzzling, but up in the high country where life can be mean and raw there are countervailing forces and experiences enough to soften the jagged edges of the struggle; thus the disproportionate number of good, sweet people in these big, wild mountains.

The people in the northern part of this territory are different in some respects from the ones in the south, but not so much in ways that matter. Those in the north speak with a bit of an accent — so say the southerners — and they don't eat much grits or cornbread in the north. But they all, everywhere, survive. This they all know how to do. They know how to keep warm in winter and cool in summer, and they rarely go hungry. Theirs is not what their neighbors outside the region would call haute cuisine, but most of the Appalachians wouldn't care much about haute cuisine anyway. But they can hustle up a bowl of fried fish or chicken that kings and queens would slobber over, and they can serve you biscuits and cornbread and hushpuppies and greens of a hundred sorts that are subliminal. From north to south they know how to use a blade and a gun, and most of them have a number of these, and they set aside money to pay for ammunition before they buy groceries or pay their taxes. With one bullet an Appalachian woman can put as much as a hundred pounds of meat in the house. Or, conversely, keep two hundred pounds out.

These people don't cotton much to style in their attire but tend more toward comfort and utility, which is really a part of surviving. Most of them wear warm coats and pants in the winter and short sleeves in the summer, without much regard to fabric and color as long as it is comfortable. One could argue that they do pay attention to style in their headgear because of the ubiquity of the duckbill cap that most of the men and many of the women wear, but because they will wear the same cap all day every day for ten or fifteen or even twenty years, it is stretching it a bit to call this headgear stylish. These caps are functional. If a man has long hair, as many do, the cap will hold it in place. If he has short hair the cap will cover it and he can dispense with combing it. And if he has little or no hair it prevents heat loss in the winter and scalp blisters in the summer. And many a cap has a ten dollar bill hidden in the inside headband that is removed only in the most extreme emergencies. Not a few of these caps have a little fishing gear attached or stashed for those very same emergencies.

These people don't like to overwork themselves. And why should they? If a man and woman have the basics — shelter, food, comfort, and maybe transportation — why should they waste their time expending energy for someone else when they could be making music or poetry or liquor (some would claim that there is no material difference), or just plain philosophizing or daydreaming? Many Appalachians consider these to be important, life-sustaining pursuits that are much more valuable than what the outsiders would impose upon them. This has consternated to no end the outside politicians and do-gooders who have spent a hundred years trying to bring the Appalachians into the modern economy. They have had some success, mainly in the liquor and associated industries, which were already well established informally anyway, and to some extent in industries that are associated with hunting and fishing. Remarkably many of these people whose only educational diploma was delivered to them when they finally completed the eighth grade can rebuild or soup up any engine that you put in front of them if it predates the electronic age, and many are catching up with that, and the outsiders have had some small success in recruiting some of these geniuses into the national racing industry. But generally these economic missions continue to fail because most of the people in this vast territory prefer not to overwork themselves, preferring instead to spend their lives living.

Many of the economic missionaries to the area have abandoned their mission and have adopted the Appalachian lifestyle after only a few years of living in the territory. In some cases this has resulted from matrimony, in others from despair in their failed missions, and in still others from enlightenment and the discovery of real living. Those who despair tend to be depressed for a time but as life moves on and their neighbors stop by and sit a spell, and bring them some fried fish or fried chicken, or a mess of pork chops and maybe an occasional jar of mountain nectar, their depression is eased and they too begin to see their community in a new light and to enjoy a more decompressed lifestyle. Once settled in, many of these renounce their mission and never leave. They put in a little garden, get a couple of pigs and rig up a pen of some sort for them in the backyard, get a dozen or so chickens, and maybe some rabbits and a couple of milk goats, and of course a duckbill cap, and they are home.

~ ~ ~

As the years and decades have become centuries, and change has come to this land, as it does to all without fail, the little spring-fed brook that starts right behind Earl Jackson's house has channeled enough water to fill a river, and it still flows, picking up volume as brooks and streams along the way join it and contribute. There are still a few cows and sheep and goats and pigs and chickens on small farms scattered around the mountains and the valleys, and homo still rises at dawn and feeds them and counts them, and claims them as his.

Earl and Jessie are still there, resting in that green field where the sheep used to graze. Jessie never left. She never, ever left. There is a fence around the plot, and there are other graves there now. One can still hear the mountain sounds of Earl's and Jessie's time, but they now compete with the roar of engines on the road and in the fields, and even in the sky.

The doves are still there and they come and they go, and frequently in the evening before the mountains darken, they fly in and alight on the fence that surrounds Earl and Jessie and they coo and they nudge each other, and again that timeless spirit spreads across the mountains and the valleys, and the creatures hush, and if one listens intently as the light fades and darkness deepens, one can still hear, as they sound that distant ancient cadence, the call of the dulcimer and the songs of the hills:

ecce homo, ecce homo

Abba, Abba

THE ZEN MAN

The archbishop, or Archie as he was called by most, was visiting an old man who had spent most of his life being. He grew most of his own food, including vegetables, pigs, chickens, corn, and a little milo. He had worked enough in his earlier years to receive a nice little monthly Social Security check, which contributed to his independence because it was more than enough given his lifestyle. But like most other people in these parts, he would still be independent even if he lost his Social Security check. He knew how to live. Archie loved these people. He had only recently met this one, and they struck it off well.

—You got any neighbors that ya think I might like to meet to help me get to know this area a little better? Archie asked.

The old man thought for a moment.

—They's a little zen man that lives about halfway down the mountain where a gushin' spring comes outta the ground. Some folks call'im the little goat man, but most of us call'im Zen. I don't know why. He come down here a good while back from somewhere away from the hills. He don't eat nothin but wild stuff and what he gits from his goats. He does keep a few chickens. Everybody around here keeps a few chickens. He rakes his yard about ever day. He totes up river gravel from the bottom a little sack full at a time and dumps it in his yard and rakes it. Done that for years. Keeps the purdiest yard. It's always got rake lines in it, and he rakes'em in purdy patterns in different patches around the place and he's got these little trails around the yard where ya can walk and not mess up his gravel, and he's got these little teenie trees next to big rocks scattered around. Don't know how he gets them little trees to look like they's grown trees. Most of the folks around here sweep their yards, but he don't do that. He rakes his yard cuz it's gravel instead of dirt and he gits them lines in it thataway. Man it's purdy. Looks almost like a midget place. Oncet or twicet a month the sheriff'll bring'im some whiskey and set a spell with'im. He usually brings'im enough till the next time. They been friends since before anybody can remember. Some folks say right after he gotchere they got in a little tussle when the sheriff went out there when Zen first showed up and bought his place. The sheriff wanted to let'im know he wuz an outsider and to let'im know who's who around here, and the sheriff pushed'im down a couple of times, and the little zen man got up and whupped the daylights outta the sheriff who was twicet his size and strong as an ox and then he helped him git up and clean off the blood with some o' that cold spring water and then the two of'em just generally rested and visited for a few minutes after he'd made sure he hat'n broke the sheriff's arm. Then the sheriff offered'im a job and Zen said Naw he'd rather just stay up here and watch the sun come up of a mornin' and the sheriff said okay he got that but he might need to deputiz'im ever now and then for special trouble and Zen said that'd be fine and the sheriff said he'd go ahead and deputize him right then for carryin' a pistol and Zen said that'd be fine but he dit'n have a pistol and the sheriff said he'd bring'im one in a week or two, which he did and a gallon jug of whiskey. They been buddies ever since. Ain't nobody messes with Zen.

Archie chuckled and said he'd love to meet Mr. Zen. The old man told Archie he would take him down to Zen's place anytime he wanted to go but he didn't think Zen was much into religion but he didn't know for sure and he didn't need to call him Mister. Archie said he wasn't much into religion either, and the old man said But everybody knows you're an archbishop. How can you not be into religion? Archie said We'll talk more about that later. Let's see if we can run down there in the morning.

Archie appreciated the Appalachian people for generally knowing how to fix their own problems. If they don't, they will figure it out. They approach each problem with a view to pushing through it or working around it. They are seldom formulaic about it. They don't need formulas; what's there is there. Deal with it. And so he could see how the sheriff would not consider it to be unusual for Zen to help him after their tussle, and for them to become fast friends. As for Zen, his problem was that he had been pushed down twice – and he needed to make sure that he was not pushed down again. So in this case, he did not attempt to work around the problem, but rather chose to push through it. As a result, he made the problem go away.

From the sheriff's point of view, he had just met a super interesting little fellow, who had whipped the daylights out of him. There was no call to be angry about this; he had simply met someone whose services he could use in the future. And besides, he was fascinated by this little fellow, who had taken him down, and then helped clean him up after the tussle. The fellow even acted like he actually liked the sheriff, which was unusual around here. Most people in these parts didn't seem to like the sheriff, although they voted him into office every time there was an election. This puzzled the sheriff, but he didn't let it bother him. Anyway, for now he had found a new buddy.

Archie looked forward to meeting Mr. Zen.

Shanky Bottom, 2024

Not far from the intersection of Virginia, Tennessee, and North Carolina, up in the big mountains, there is a community by a river, if one can call it that, known as Shanky Bottom. There are few communities in this land bearing the name Shanky, although you will find one over in middle Tennessee by Kentucky in Clay County, but that is not our Shanky.

There is a bar in Shanky Bottom called Shanky Bar. Shanky Bar is the only bar in Shanky Bottom. Indeed it is the only commercial establishment in Shanky Bottom, although Louise Shanky Purcell's back bedroom has been called a commercial establishment from time to time, but more about that in a moment.

The bar is an establishment where the locals can procure just about anything they desire, including food, drink, financial services of sorts, and high speed Internet with downloads at 24 mbps, and uploads at 4 mbps, although in Shanky Bottom the upload capacity is seldom used. Shanky folk and their neighbors and customers tend more toward media consumption than content creation.

The community consists of eight habitations grouped within the bottom, housing forty to fifty souls, most of whom are kin within the third or fourth degrees of consanguinity, which may also be said of the general population on the surrounding mountains. There is another establishment near the houses, but technically it is not in Shanky Bottom but is rather in the woods in a draw that lies off the bottom and runs a few hundred yards into the hills. There is nothing that the taxing authorities would call a road leading to it, but the operators of this establishment have no trouble hauling grain and sugar up the draw with a mule or tractor wagon. There is a lively spring that never goes dry that flows from the hillside down into the draw, providing pure mountain water for the best whiskey made anywhere in these parts, or at least within five miles of the bottom, and this is saying much because the competition in these hills is fierce.

Some of this mountain nectar is served to the patrons of Shanky Bar upon special request, but only to those who are regulars and whom the proprietors of the bar have known for decades. These proprietors are the patriarchs and matriarchs of the bottom and the surrounding mountains, and the family extends far beyond the few souls who live in the bottom itself. The bar, and this extended family, have a wholesome relationship with the two banks in Shanky Mountain, the nearby town, and with the town's feed store, owned by some Shanky cousins, which sells far more corn than the local livestock, domestic and feral, could possibly consume, and which several years back added sugar to its inventory. There is a railroad spur at the feed store that offloads directly into the side of the store's warehouse, and after the rail company started delivering sugar by the carload, the feds called the sheriff and asked her what was up with all the sugar going into town. They said that the Department of Commerce had a database somewhere on the East Coast that kept track of all sugar sales in the world and that they had never seen so much sugar being sold to such a small community of people anywhere on the planet. The sheriff listened politely and then she explained that these hill people needed a lot of extra sugar to get them through the harsh winters, and also they used a lot of sugar in the cooking of their jams and preserves that they sold to the thousands of tourists who came through each fall to view the beautiful mountain color. The feds expressed some doubts about such a large number of tourists who would visit a town that didn't even appear on most maps and that their own agents had a hard time finding. They mumbled something about how there weren't enough people in the town including within fifty miles of it to consume that much sugar no matter how cold the winter was, but they left it at that, at least for a while. From past experience they had concluded that shutting down the local manufacture of distilled spirits in these hills was impossible given the lack of assistance from the local law enforcement authorities and financial institutions. Even the local preachers kindly told the feds that they didn't see how they could help them with this problem.

Now, back to Louise's back bedroom. It is a place of comfort and rest, a place where one can find relief when it is not to be found anywhere else. Louise herself is a bit of an enigma. She graduated from grammar school in the nearby town, quite an accomplishment back in the day, and moved out of the bottom to attend high school several mountains away where her third cousin on her mama's side lived and where a room was made available to her for the four years of high school being as how she was kin. She then moved down to Chapel Hill, got herself admitted, and spent the next eight years waiting tables and grinding her way through school. She left with a bachelor of science degree and a doctorate in medicine, graduating second in her class, and headed off to Oxford, England where she had been admitted to a one-year internship in a hospital there with the prospect of an Oxon masters degree if she presented an acceptable thesis at the end of the year and successfully completed the internship with a few academic courses scattered in. Those were still the days when an intern may have slept a total of a hundred nights during the year of the internship. But she plowed through, meeting her objective; and leaving the year behind in a dim fog, and following her DNA, she left her stuff in Oxford and made her way up to Scotland to find a mountain where she could stay in a little hut and have a good, hard, three-day cry. Louise missed Shanky Bottom. She really missed Shanky Bottom. It was almost as if her soul had separated from her and was now in Shanky Bottom and she could see it there thousands of miles away and she was nothing here because her soul was there, not here. But how can you see a soul? I can see it, she told herself, that's me, that's me there, I don't have a soul here any more, my soul's in Shanky Bottom, and she cried some more.

So Dr. Louise Purcell went back home. She joined a little clinic which served as the hospital in the town near Shanky Bottom and she treated the general population, stitching cuts, setting bones, prescribing and dispensing nose drops and cough medicine, and delivering babies. There were eight beds in the clinic which was right next door to the doctor who owned it, and at the rear there was a tiny apartment intended as lodging for any staff whose overnight presence might be required. The doctor who owned the clinic offered this lodging to Louise, but she insisted on living in her old home place in Shanky Bottom, which her mother had deeded to her the day after she returned from Great Britain. Her house had four bedrooms. She and her mother occupied two of them, and her daddy stayed drunk in the third. And then there was the fourth, the back bedroom.

Of the four bedrooms, this was the only one that had a door leading out of the house. It had its own tiny porch, just big enough for two rocking chairs and a small table between them. A guest could sit there and observe the critters in the back yard and enjoy a mountain evening without being seen by travelers on the road in front of the house. And of course an occupant of this back bedroom could enter and leave the house without being seen by those in other parts of the house or out in the front yard. This room had its own plumbing, installed in what may have been a sewing room or a pantry when some of the earlier Shanky family built the house. There was a ceramic thing plumbed between the toilet and the lavatory that puzzled almost everyone who saw it. It was oblong and looked like a cross between the toilet and the sink. It had a spigot but it did not have the flushing capability of a toilet and it was too low to function as a normal sink. Because this thing was so unusual and nobody knew what to make of it, everybody in Shanky Bottom knew about it and had seen it, having by right of tribe been given a tour of the john, and most people in the nearby town and on the surrounding mountains had heard about it and had included it in their lore. One of the more affluent Shanky boys had brought it back from France for his mama, Louise's grandma, after he had spent some time studying there. Unfortunately, he left for Abilene before he could educate the locals about it, and he never came back. The only clue that he had left about the thing was that it was supposed to be called a biddit, as in what one does at an auction for an item that one wants to buy, he explained, as he attempted to teach the pronunciation of the thing, but this confused the locals even more because after the boy installed it for his mama and left Shanky Bottom, the Shankys first put it to use by designating the back bedroom as a place to gather and rinse their garden produce, in this thing, and these locals couldn't figure out what rinsing vegetables had to do with an auction. Such was the state of affairs when Louise Purcell returned from Oxford and settled back into her old home place in

Shanky Bottom. One day later she owned the house and the thing, and she determined to repurpose the back bedroom.

Everybody needs a place to cry, Louise told herself. All of God's children cry, or at least should. Homo cries, and Homo laughs. She determined that she would offer her fourth bedroom as a place of comfort for souls who needed it, and as a place for contemplation and perhaps even isolation for souls who might need that. Her thinking came from experience.

So Dr. Lou, as she had become known in these mountains, put a simple single bed in the room. She had the furniture store bring her another chifforobe and put it in what she called the comfort room. She loved this kind of furniture; it had a tall closet-like section on the left, a little over five feet high, and a set of four drawers on the right at the top of which was a flat surface, a little over waist high, with an adjustable mirror at the back. In the closet portion on the left there was room to hang dresses, suits, or other long items, and the drawers to the right provided ample space for a visitor to store whatever might be needed for a brief sojourn. She loved the minimalism of this furniture. She completed the furnishing with a simple table and two straight-back chairs, an old roll top desk that she picked up for almost nothing, and a comfortable stuffed chair. She left the bathroom as it was, including the bidet and the clawfoot bathtub. Shanky Bottom now had a mental health facility that over the years would serve troubled souls, including the mighty and the mini — a United States senator, a governor, university presidents, a world renowned poet, painters, and many others, known and unknown, who needed a place of rest and comfort that sometimes can be found only in solitude, a place where they can cry and reflect and suffer and quietly pass through the valley of the shadow of death. This was Dr. Lou's back bedroom in Shanky Bottom.

The Cross Burnings on Cherokee Ridge

Minnie Fletcher

The night of the first cross burning on Cherokee Ridge, well past midnight of a warm night in May, three men knocked on Minnie Fletcher's door to request her services. Miss Minnie got out of bed and put on a house robe and came to the door. Such late night calls were not unusual for Miss Minnie.

She lived in a house out at the edge of town where she grew her garden and kept a milk cow and some laying hens and raised a few pigs each year, like most people in these parts. But also like everybody on the mountain she needed at least some income, so she provided a most unusual service. Miss Minnie could talk the fire out of you.

Everybody on the mountain knew that if you got burned the most expedient and the cheapest way to get relief was to go to Miss Minnie. Her emergency room was wherever she chose to see you when you got there; sometimes it would be her porch, sometimes her living room, sometimes her kitchen, sometimes her garden. It didn't matter, and she took all comers. Miss Minnie always said there was no charge for her services because it was God that gave her the ability to "talk the far outcha", but almost everybody who came for help left a few coins on her porch or the kitchen table when they left. Those who didn't have any coins to leave would come back in a few days with a string of fish, or a rabbit they had just caught and dressed, or other produce of the mountain, including an occasional pint jar of a clear liquid that just about everybody around these parts appreciated, including Miss Minnie.

Miss Minnie's place was the only fully integrated institution on the mountain at the time. If a Negro was there first and then a Cherokee and then a hifalutin White Man arrived, the order in which she performed her healing art was Negro, Cherokee, hifalutin White Man. Everyone was fine with that. Her place was neutral territory; those who came to her place came for relief from pain. They did not come to fight or to belittle anyone else who might be there, and so she was able to provide her services to all who came, and she never refused her services to anyone. She would even let these people use the telephone that hung on the wall in her living room next to the kitchen door. This was completely out of the question for most white people on the mountain; they would not allow Negroes or Cherokee to talk into their telephone for fear of catching something.

If the burn was blistered real bad, or if the skin was gone and you could see the quick, Miss Minnie would go ahead and talk the pain out of you and smear some lard or butter on the wound and then send you to the doctor so he could work on you and try to keep you from getting infected. She couldn't do anything about infection. Even the doctors in town recognized that her ministrations were as successful as theirs, and perhaps even more successful, with burns that didn't destroy the skin. The consensus in the medical community was that somehow Miss Minnie had acquired the ability to hypnotize; since she frequently sent bad burns to the hospital or to local physicians, they respected her and accepted her as a healer. They simply could not argue with her results. Unlike these licensed professional healers, however, Miss Minnie owed no duty of secrecy or confidentiality to anyone.

Miss Minnie flipped the porch light on and looked through the screen at the three men standing at her front door.

"Howdy Miss Minnie. I'm Johnny Mitchell from over on Mitchell's Ridge. This here's Milton and he just got his hand burned purdy bad and he needs for ya to talk the far outn' it if ya will. This here other fella's a friend o' ours from over in Barlow County. Name's Lester."

She looked at their faces in the porch light; she didn't know any of them. She opened the screen door. "Come on in and take a seat here in the living room. I'll be back in a minute."

Miss Minnie went into her bedroom and shut the door; she took her chamber pot from under her bed and squatted on it. The men could hear her urinating. After a few moments she came back into the living room and motioned for Johnny to pull up a chair by hers and have Milton sit.

"Hold your hand out here so I can see it."

She looked carefully. The burn covered his entire hand. Skin had already started peeling away from the quick. Milton was agitated but he was trying to control himself and not show his pain.

"This is pretty bad. What happened?"

"We wuz just having some fun over at one of the Cherokee farms and Milton spilled some gas on his hand when he wuz splashin' it on the cross, and then when he struck the match his hand and his sleeve caught far – just kinda flashed right up and then kept on burning. He was jumping around screaming still standing right next to the cross so several of us jumped on him and jerked him away so the rest of'im wouldn' catch on far."

Miss Minnie looked at Milton's face and attempted to look into his eyes but he looked away. She began passing her hand in a circular motion over his hand and chanting in a low voice. She finally was able to look Milton in the eye as she continued chanting for several minutes. Milton began to calm down and after awhile he appeared to be no longer in pain. Lester watched.

"Shore looks like he's better," Lester said to Johnny. "But I betcha he won't be strikin' the matches over at the Rogers place tomorrow night. That hand's a mess." He grinned and looked at Milton's hand and then at Miss Minnie. Two of his front teeth were missing, one on top and one on the bottom. He looked proudly at Johnny. Johnny glared at him.

The Rogers place was a little farm over on Cherokee Ridge just outside of Cherokee Town, a grouping of habitations where some of the Cherokee people lived and had their gardens and backyard livestock. Some claimed that those Rogers were part of the same roots as the Will Rogers family out in Oklahoma but nobody ever bothered to trace it back. The Cherokee people on our mountain were descendants of those who had avoided the forced removal to the western Indian lands a hundred years before, either by hiding or by exemption because they lived on private lands instead of Indian lands. Their number had increased considerably since the Trail of Tears; they were now back up to about five percent of the total population. They were good hard-working folk that stayed out of trouble and took care of their own. Miss Minnie had talked the fire out of many of them over the years, and over the years some of their old people had taught her many of their herbal remedies.

"No, I don't believe he will either," Miss Minnie said as she stood. "Wait here a minute while I go mix'im up a lard salve to rub over it till he can go to the doctor. But before I do ya'll need to listen to me – he needs to go straight from here to the doctor 'cause that hand can get bad infected. We can go ahead and call the doctor now. Ya'll can use my phone."

"I'll letcha put the lard on, but I ain't gonna be goin' to no doctor," Milton said.

Miss Minnie glanced at Milton and with a nod and the faintest hint of a smile she stepped into her kitchen. She returned a few minutes later with a paper cup in her hand.

"I've fixed you up some burn salve here. Your hand won't hurt for another ten or fifteen minutes after you leave here. You need to let your hand be calming for another five minutes or so after you leave here and then take a blob of this here salve in your good hand and smear it all over your burned hand real quick so it won't hurt so bad while you're rubbing it on. If it's hurtin' too bad, get one of these here boys to rub it on for you. But it shouldn' be hurtin' yet at that point. And you be sure you go straight from here to the doctor. He'll give you something for your pain when you get there. You can get to the hospital from here easy in fifteen or twenty minutes."

"I'll rub it on myself and I ain't goin' to no doctor. My mama used to use butter. You sure this lard'll work?"

Miss Minnie handed him the paper cup containing the salve. "It'll work."

The men stood and Johnny laid four quarters on the table next to the lamp.

"I'm tellin' ya now young man, you're gonna need to see a doctor for that hand less'n you want to lose it."

Milton smirked, and the men got in their pickup truck and left.

Miss Minnie picked up the phone and called the hospital and told the shift nurse in the emergency room that a young man with a badly burned hand would be arriving in about forty-five minutes. The nurse asked her why it would take so long for them to get there being as how her place wasn't fifteen minutes from the hospital. Miss Minnie told her it was because they weren't going to be going there straight from her place, that they were heading out to Mitchell's Ridge first but after about twenty minutes of driving they would be turning around and heading back into town to go to the hospital. She said they would be driving a lot faster coming back into town so they should be arriving at the hospital in just about forty-five minutes.

Johnny drove out of town and soon the men were on the narrow curving roads leading to Mitchell's Ridge and Johnny's place where the men were staying. They didn't speak. After about five minutes of hard driving and a few miles down the road, Johnny pulled over and stopped.

"You want me to rub that salve on ya?"

"Naw, I'll do it. Here, hold this cup."

Milton took a blob of the salve about the size of an egg in his left hand and quickly rubbed it all over his burned hand, and thoroughly between his fingers. It didn't hurt.

"She shore nuff knew what she was doing ditn she?" said Lester. "That's the first time I seen anybody talk the far outta somebody."

When Milton had thoroughly coated his hand with Miss Minnie's salve, Johnny pulled back onto the road and drove on toward his place. Within a few minutes Milton started breathing in deeply and exhaling deeply and making grunting and moaning noises that the others could hear over the sounds of the truck. A few moments later he began to flail around in the pickup. He was sitting in the middle between Johnny and Lester and suddenly he leaned over in front of Lester to hold his hand out the window in the wind. After another minute or so he began to yell. Johnny asked him if he wanted to go back to Miss Minnie's for some more talking and Milton said he never wanted to go there again, that she hadn't done him any good at all except for just a few minutes and that now he was hurtin' worse than when he went to her house and that in fact he was hurtin' worse than he had ever hurt in his life.

Johnny drove on and after two or three minutes Milton had completely lost his composure – he was jumping around wildly inside the cab, constantly yelling. He crawled onto Lester's lap to get his hand farther out into the wind and stayed there until Lester finally managed to get out from under him and move to the middle next to Johnny. None of the men had ever experienced this much activity in the cab of a pickup truck, and by now Johnny's main concern was to keep from running off the road and wrecking the truck.

Suddenly Milton yelled that he needed to see a doctor. Johnny yelled back that they were a good twenty to thirty minutes from the nearest doctor, which would be the emergency room doctor, and that he might not even be there at this time of night but might have to be waked up and called in, and besides, he had just said that he watn' gonna go see no doctor. Milton yelled back that under the circumstances he had changed his mind and that now he did want to see a doctor and that he didn't care what the doctor was doing he needed to see'im right now.

That settled it. Johnny slowed and did a U-turn and sped back toward the hospital in town. Milton kept his hand out in the wind and yelled and bounced all the way to the hospital. When they pulled up to the emergency room the duty nurse was dozing at her desk but Milton's screams woke her. She took a quick look at Milton's greasy hand and said, "I'm going to have to call the doctor. It'll be about twenty minutes before he can get here."

"Jesus God Almighty woman! I cain't wait no twenty minutes. Why the hell don't ya'll keep a doctor here all the time? Don't you know a man might need to come see a doctor any time of the day or night?" He was still screaming.

The nurse looked at his hand again and appeared to be a little woozy herself. "There's a colored doctor already here in the hospital over on their side, but you probably don't want to go over there do you?"

Milton yelled back that he just needed to see a doctor that it didn't matter what part of the hospital he was in that what mattered was his pain and that he needed to do something right now not in twenty minutes. He was jumping around and holding his right wrist with his left hand and bending forward as if bowing and then standing back up and then bending his knees and grimacing and then straightening up, as he screamed and yelled. Down the hall a couple of heads popped out of their rooms and stared toward the emergency area.

"He looks like he's really hurting," the nurse said to Johnny and Lester.

"Yes Ma'am, it shore seems so. It wuz all I could do to drive'im here with him a jumpin' around inside the truck and makin' such a fuss the whole way."

The nurse managed to get Milton into a wheel chair and rolled him through the dividing doors and into the colored section of the hospital emergency department with Milton yelling and kicking his legs as she pushed him down the hall. Milton was still hollering when Dr. Allison helped the nurse put him on an examining table and looked closely at Milton's hand. He spoke to the nurse and a few seconds later she handed Dr. Allison a syringe. He found a vein and gave him the injection and within a few moments Milton was sedated. The doctor examined the dark brown salve that thickly coated his patient's burned hand. He lifted the hand and leaned forward and smelled the salve and then asked the nurse to bring the other two men in and when they arrived he asked them what had happened.

"Milton burned his hand." Johnny left out the part about the cross burning.

"I'd say it sure looks like he burned his hand."

The doctor knew that he wasn't going to get any more useful information about the burn from these boys.

"We taken'im over to Miss Minnie's to get the far talked out'n it and she did it and it worked. But she told'im he needed to see a doctor right away 'cause of the infection, and he said he watn' gonna go see no doctor. She mixed'im up a salve and told'im to wait a few minutes 'fore puttin' it on and he did it just the way she said. We'uz two or three miles down the road 'fore Milton rubbed the salve on his burned hand real good. But it watn' long after he smeared on the salve that he started yelling and screaming and beatin' around inside the truck and stickin' his hand out the window, and then he decided to come to the hospital."

Dr. Allison thanked Johnny and Lester and sent them back over to the white side and picked up the phone and called Miss Minnie.

"Miss Minnie, this is Dr. Allison. Sorry to have to call you at three o'clock in the morning."

"That's okay. I've been waitin' up for a call from y'all."

"Miss Minnie, there's a man here with a burned hand, and the men with him say that you talked the fire out of him a little while ago."

"Yes I did Dr. Allison. It worked real good, and I told him that he was still gonna need to see a doctor right now because it was a real bad burn. I could already see the quick all over his hand and between his fingers. But he said he wasn't gonna go see no doctor, so I mixed him up a little burn salve in some lard that would cover his burned hand real good and kill the germs."

"Yes I saw the coating on his hand, and what did you put in the salve Miss Minnie?"

"Well, just things that I knew would kill the germs, like salt and snuff and cayenne pepper powder."

"Yes, I thought it was something like that. I thought I smelled the snuff."

"Yes Sir. They mentioned something about a burning at the Rogers place tomorrow night, Dr. Allison, and I just felt like this hand really needed to be treated before they did something like that."

He paused, sensing that she was telling him something.

"Yes Miss Minnie. And how much of this salt and snuff and cayenne pepper powder did you use?"

"Well, I used about a cup of lard, didn't put any butter in it – butter's been kinda scarce here lately since my cow dried up – and I put a heaping tablespoon each of the salt and snuff and cayenne pepper powder. Then I mixed it all together real good, and then I mixed in a little bit of Pinee so it would smell like a salve ought to. And they say the Pinee'll kill germs too and keep flies off to boot. Don't you think that was about right Dr. Allison?"

He hadn't seen this particular formulation in his materia medica classes at Harvard Medical School but he would certainly have to agree with her science. She knew without a doubt that the application of this salve would get this man to the hospital and would prompt a call to her from the attending physician. These mountain people often amazed him. What would have happened if he had not been the doctor on duty this night? Surely most of the doctors would do precisely what he was going to do; but if not, certainly Miss

Minnie would have taken the next step and notified someone who would know what to do. Obviously her objective was to communicate the information about the plans for the Rogers place without compromising her neutrality, but he was satisfied that she would have done whatever was necessary to get the message out.

Like most doctors on the mountain he moonlighted in the emergency department for a few shifts each month, and he saw some strange things; but this thing with Miss Minnie was a first for him.

"Yes Miss Minnie, I think that was just about right. Yes Ma'am. Well, we always appreciate you, Miss Minnie. If you ever need anything you let me know. You get yourself some rest now, and thank you. I'll take care of it from here."

He cradled the telephone and walked back to his patient and checked his pulse. He would keep him sedated for a few hours – at least until the doctor for the next shift arrived. He would get a nurse in here to clean the salve off the patient's hand while he was sedated. The other boys could wait on the white side. He would get a message to them later in the morning. Now he needed to get a message to the Rogers family, and he was pretty sure they didn't have a telephone. The day shift doctor who would relieve him would be arriving shortly. He sensed that big trouble lay ahead.

JOHNNY WOLF

D r. Allison left the hospital at six o'clock when the doctor taking the next shift arrived. He stopped by his house and told his wife he would be late for breakfast, then drove to his preacher's house. The preacher was up and cooking breakfast; he poured Dr. Allison a cup of coffee. The doctor told the preacher what had happened in the emergency room and what Miss Minnie had said about the Rogers place and the burning that was to take place there that evening. He finished his coffee and declined the preacher's offer of breakfast, and upon the preacher's assurance that he would get the message to the Cherokee as soon as he finished eating, Dr. Allison drove home and had another cup of coffee and breakfast with his wife.

When he finished eating, the preacher drove out to Cherokee Ridge and found Johnny Wolf. It was already a hot morning late in May. School would be out for the summer in less than two weeks. But for now the preacher knew that Johnny would be leaving for school in a few minutes. This was the second message that the preacher had received this morning. A man came over from Free Town – the Colored section of town, known by many as Nigger Town, at the edge of which the preacher lived – and told him that word was getting around that the Klan was bragging about how they were going to burn down a Cherokee house somewhere tonight, but nobody knew which one. Now he had the connection.

"There's gonna be trouble tonight Johnny. Just wanted to let you know."

"What's happening Preacher?"

"Word's out that some of the Klan are gonna burn the Rogers place tonight, not just a cross."

Johnny looked out over the valley below Cherokee Town. For some time now he had felt that something like this was coming. For months the Klan had been making noises about the Cherokee. They had even slashed some Cherokee tires and had shot two of their dogs. He could feel the evil coming.

"Thank ya Preacher. We'll take care of it. Looks like the time's come. Lord willin' we'll return the favor to you and your folks soon." The old black man looked at him and made a little nod but said nothing. Johnny watched him walk to his car. He loved these people almost as much as he loved his Cherokee people.

Johnny was a man of small stature in his early forties who was generally recognized as the leader of the Cherokee people on the mountain. He had graduated from the white high school and had gone down to Chapel Hill and worked his way through a four-year degree in seven years, sweeping the floors of Old East and flipping burgers in the cafeteria and various cafes and restaurants around town. He finally got a white jacket job at the Carolina Inn where he worked until he graduated, building up his cash reserves from the generous tips he received from affluent diners. He came back to the mountain with more money than he had taken with him seven years earlier. He took over the coaching job at the Negro high school and taught social studies there. Johnny was one of those rare souls who wanted to earn just enough to meet his basic needs and nothing more. He had forsworn the pursuit of money beyond his basic needs to pursue his mission, and this empowered him in the sense that he was free from many of the burdens and constraints imposed upon someone who was driven by money.

Johnny took a great interest in the sociology of the mountain. The segregation had always disgusted him, and he had determined that no man would diminish his humanity because he was not a Caucasian. Before he left Chapel Hill to return to the mountain he had already made a commitment to resist racist assaults against his people and the Negroes using whatever means might be necessary. He had decided that no matter what happened because of his race when he returned to the mountain, or how painful it might be, he would never back down. If he had to spill his own blood to have the freedom that he envisaged for his people and the coloreds so be it.

The preacher's news made him angry. For years he had wondered what it was about these people that made it possible for them to harm other people because of the color of their skin. No matter how you viewed it, no matter that this mountain was mostly populated with good people, there was here – as there was just about everywhere – a spirit of evil that existed side by side with the good. It was a spirit that wormed its way into a man and took him over and made him less than what humans are supposed to be, and it drove him to do things that destroyed innocent people's lives. It hadn't been ten years ago that the Klan had lynched a twelve year old Negro boy right outside of town. They claimed he had whistled at a fifteen year old white girl. For decades they had burned down houses and shot dogs and livestock that belonged to Negroes, and neither this sheriff nor the one before him nor the one before that one ever did anything about it. They never did *anything* about it! They would tell the Negro man or the Cherokee man to let the law take its course. Fools! How can an intelligent man tell them this when the law never did anything for them when they were the victims? What law? He knew as most real men know that there comes a time in a man's life when he just has to take a stand and take action, and let the consequences be what they will. Sometimes the law just doesn't work. That's when a man has to appeal to a higher law, and Johnny knew what he was going to do. Two hundred years was long enough. The time had come.

~ ~ ~

Johnny thought about what the Klan apparently had planned for tonight. But whoever had made the decision for the Klan to come to the Rogers place tonight had made a major mistake. There was not a Cherokee on the whole mountain who had the slightest fear of these Klan imbeciles. He could not fathom why they would risk assaulting his people, other than that they were quite simply stupid. The truth was, they were not the mountain rabble; they were mostly average people – farmers, mechanics, day laborers who considered themselves better than others because they were Caucasians. That was certainly their call, but one thing was for sure: there would be unhappy white women on the mountain in the morning. The Klan might be able to use fear and intimidation to control people in some places, but it wasn't going to happen here on Cherokee Ridge.

Johnny finished his coffee and got in his pickup and drove out toward the Rogers house. He had an hour and a half before he had to be at school. He stopped at several houses along the way and told the men to meet him at the Rogers farm at noon to discuss a community emergency. Knowing their attitude toward the clock – the people around here called it Indian time – he asked them to be there right at noon because he was on the government clock. This would give them time to finish their morning tasks, and since he didn't have cafeteria duty this week he could leave school for an hour or so to meet with the men. They told him they would be there at noon.

The Klan had started disputing with the Cherokee people several months back, saying that white folk were racially superior to the Cherokees and that the Indians didn't have any business being around the white folks just like the niggers didn't. And the Cherokees said that's fine. This aggravated some of the Klan members so the Klan said they would deal with the Indians just like they dealt with the niggers, and they picked out a family of Cherokees and put on their white robes and hoods and went over to that family's house one night and put a cross in the yard and started burning it. The problem for the Klan was that this midnight burning didn't scare the Cherokee. So the Klan put out word they were going to do some burning at somebody else's house the next night and they didn't intend to limit it to a cross this time. This didn't scare the Cherokee either.

It would not have been the first time that the Klan had burned down a house on the mountain. In fact over the years they had torched several houses and barns and other structures, including a church or two, that belonged to black folk. Johnny made a decision this morning that the Klan had committed its last burning on this mountain.

There was a crowd of Cherokee men at the Rogers house just after noon. Johnny guessed eighteen or twenty at first glance. He told the men what the preacher had told him earlier.

"I'm going to send the Rogers women to somebody else's house right after supper this evening, and I'm comin' up here with my 22 rifle and my 30-30 and two or three boxes of ammo for each one of'em. I'm gonna wait for these imbeciles. When they get here and light the fire the first thing I'm gonna do is shoot as many of'em in the legs as I can, and then I'm gonna shoot the lights out of their vehicles and I'm gonna shoot their tires, and when I've done that I'm gonna start shooting their windshields and their radiators and any other parts of them trucks that I can hit from where I'm shooting. I'm not going to try to kill anybody, but I'm gonna put a hurtin' on'em.

"Any of y'all that want to can join me. I think we need to put a stop to this nonsense before it gets started. How many of you think you can be here tonight?"

Every man there said he would be back by dark with a rifle and plenty of ammo.

"Alright. About half of you bring 22's for shooting their legs and the rest of you bring your huntin' rifles for shootin' the vehicles. I've got to get on to the schoolhouse so y'all work that out before you leave.

"When you get here take that tractor path past the house and park in that little field back behind those woods and come on back up to the house. We'll wait behind the bushes till we see'em comin'. Everybody bring some short pieces of rope for tourniquets. We'll probably need'em."

The night of the second and last cross burning on Cherokee Ridge, around midnight, the men who had gathered at the Rogers house saw the headlights of the Klan cars and pickups snaking up the curves of the farm road to the house. The Cherokee had taken positions where the Klansmen couldn't see them when their headlights shone on the house. The Klansmen jumped out of their vehicles and set up the cross in the Rogers' front yard and set it afire, and once the cross was in full blaze a white robe ran up to the cross and lit a torch with it and threw the burning torch onto the front porch. One of the Cherokee men jumped onto the porch, grabbed the torch and threw it back into the crowd of white robes.

"Now!" Johnny yelled, and the Cherokees who had the 22 caliber rifles started shooting the Klansmen in the legs, aiming about knee high; and the ones with the high powered rifles shot at all the cars and pickups. They shot out the lights and tires of every Klan car and pickup there except for one or two at the rear of the group of vehicles which managed to turn around quickly and drive away and even they had bullet holes in them. For two or three minutes the sound of the gunfire was like the finale of the fireworks at the annual county fair.

White robes scattered everywhere and men were screaming. The Cherokees stopped shooting and let all the men that still had functioning legs run into the woods and make their way back to wherever they came from. The Cherokee men went out and checked on the men that were lying on the ground or crawling around in the yard. They pulled the hoods off all of them. They knew most of them. One of the men lying in the yard moaning was a deputy sheriff that everybody on the mountain knew. Both his legs were a mangled mess from the knees down, shot all to pieces; and he had a small caliber rifle wound in each hand that he had received when he had instinctively tried to block the rifle fire with his hands. And to top it off one of the pickups that had managed to leave had run right over his legs as he lay moaning in the driveway.

~   ~   ~

There were seventeen disabled vehicles, every one of which had shotguns or rifles, or both, and several boxes of ammunition in it. Everybody on the mountain that had a vehicle drove around with a gun in it – that was normal here – but these Klansmen were known for carrying around a lot more firepower than other folk.

~   ~   ~

"Get their guns and ammo." Johnny walked among the injured, looking at each man's face.

The other men checked each Klansman for injuries. Several of the men gathered the guns and ammo from the Klan vehicles and piled them in the Rogers' pickup truck while others applied tourniquets.

"Whatcha got?" Johnny asked.

"Looks like fifty-seven long guns and a hundred and twenty somethin' boxes of ammo – I ain't counted the pistols yet, but there's a pile of'em – I'd say about thirty," said the man who was stacking the guns and ammo. "Where we gonna take'em?"

"Nigger Town."

"Jesus!" moaned a bleeding Klansman.

Johnny looked at him and smiled. "Sweetheart, you'da been better off calling on Jesus before comin' out here tonight. I betcha anything he'd a tried to tell ya not to commit this foolishness."

"We're gonna divide'em up 'bout equal for all the colored churches over there in town and let the preachers give'em out." Johnny spoke loud enough for the moaning men to hear him. "I'm sure you ladies'd be welcome to attend some of their services and ask for your guns back. They probly won't even make you sit on the back row. That'd be my guess. I don't think they'll give ya your guns back though. I imagine most of you girls are familiar with the ancient maxim 'To the victor go the spoils' and as you can see we're the victor here tonight so these guns and ammo belong to us now; they're our spoils and we can give them to anybody we please. And it will please us to know that your colored neighbors have in their possession a reasonable amount of guns and ammo for the foreseeable future. Course y'all can file a complaint with the sheriff if ya want to. But one thing's for sure – we don't plan to have any more cross burnings on this mountain. You think y'all could agree?" Johnny asked sweetly.

Most of the wounded men just continued to moan, and bleed. The Cherokee men moved about the men, examining them and tightening tourniquets as needed.

After they had done what they considered necessary to prevent any deaths, all of them, including the male members of the Rogers family, got into their vehicles and left. Somebody in the bunch stopped at one of the Cherokee houses on the ridge that had a telephone and called the sheriff's office and told them what had happened and to go get the people that had been shot and told them to have the vehicles moved off the Cherokee farm by sundown the next day because they were all coming back to the Rogers place at dark and would totally destroy any vehicle that was still there.

Within a couple of hours the Rescue Squad's two ambulances had delivered fifteen men with shot up legs to the emergency room that was designed to handle no more than three people at a time. Some of the men had to be put over in the Negro part of the hospital and a colored doctor worked on them. By the time they had all been treated and admitted, everybody on the mountain knew what had happened. The next day many businesses were closed and many farms unplowed. There were even two substitute teachers called in at the white high school. The school records reflected that the two regular teachers had been accidentally wounded in the legs while coon hunting the night before.

The Cherokee family returned home the night after the second cross burning with a crowd of friends and resumed their normal routine. The Cherokees on the mountain never had any further trouble from the Klan, and the sheriff never brought any charges against the Indians, who couldn't have cared less, or the Klansmen, but he did fire the deputy who had been shot up. The colored doctor had had to amputate both his legs about six inches below the knees to save his life, so he couldn't have worked as a deputy anyway. That deputy swore that he would still have his legs if a white doctor had worked on him. Daddy said that he would still have his legs if he hadn't gone out to that Cherokee farm wearing a white robe and a hood.

As it turned out, many of those who had been able to flee had been shot and had small caliber bullet wounds in their legs. They trickled into the emergency room and various doctors' offices over the next few days as infections set in and their home remedies failed. For the next week two or three Cherokee men hung out at the entrance to the emergency room and near the entrance to each of the various doctors' offices in town, and smiled encouragingly when one of the injured men hobbled in or was carried in by his family. In most cases they knew the injured men, and wrote their names down in a notebook as they entered the doctor's office or the emergency room. At the end of the week they turned all these names over to Johnny Wolf, who enlisted the assistance of some Cherokee high school girls to write, in the name of the Cherokee community, a get well card to each of the injured men and his family, including the two teachers who had gone coon hunting.

The towing company had worked all the next day following the second cross burning on Cherokee Ridge moving the seventeen vehicles off the Cherokee farm. The sheriff had told the towing company that every one of the vehicles better be gone by sundown. The two body shops in town stayed busy for the next three weeks plugging holes and replacing radiators and headlights and windshields. One of the shops was slowed down considerably because one of its men was in the hospital with a crushed knee cap and other leg injuries that he sustained while he too was coon hunting. By the end of the three weeks most of the medical staff on the mountain concluded that there must have been an influx of coons this spring the likes of which this mountain had never experienced. When one innocent medical novice indelicately questioned the reported cause of the injury of one of his patients, noting that one usually shoots upward into trees when coon hunting at night, not toward the ground where legs usually reside, several of the mountain sages suggested that there must be a new species of ground-hugging coon that had been brought in from out west where there weren't any trees and thus the coons didn't know how to climb them.

It would be difficult to describe accurately the hilarity of the Cherokee when this explanation appeared in the Saturday edition of the newspaper. Although the Cherokee are not often celebratory by nature, when this explanation was offered in the newspaper they were moved to declare a barbeque of four full grown pigs, which they gleefully denoted as ground coons, and to this barbeque on the courthouse square, or more accurately *in* the courthouse square because they dug a long barbeque pit for the cooking, they invited the whole Cherokee community, all of whom came, and all the black preachers and Miss Minnie and the sheriff, who also came. When someone pointed out that these pigs bore only the slightest resemblance to coons, for example they had four legs, a head, and a tail, the Cherokee solemnly noted that they were indeed like this new race of coons in two important respects: the pigs, like these new ground coons, could not climb trees; and when you shot them to dress them out for human consumption, you shot them in the head right between the eyes which is at about the same level as a human knee no matter how big the pig; this required that a man standing upright shoot downward as in the shooting of this new species of coon. The mountain seemed satisfied with this explanation.

The Cherokee drafted a special invitation to the barbeque for the men and their families whose names had been noted at the entrances to the emergency room and the various medical offices within the days following the incident at the Rogers house; none of the men came, but most of their women came and were warmly received by the Cherokee. The deputy whose legs had been amputated didn't have a woman, so following the barbeque and festivities on the courthouse lawn one of the Cherokee women packed up a meal and took it to him. When she brought the meal to him he got mad. She ignored his anger as she unpacked the meal. Then he started bawling. She put her hand on his shoulder and calmed him. Because both his hands were still heavily bandaged she started feeding him the barbeque and the slaw and the hush puppies, and finally he settled down and finished the meal. The next day she brought him another meal, and this continued daily for several months. He got some artificial limbs and she helped him learn to walk on them. A week before Christmas she took him home with her and married him in front of most of the people from Cherokee Ridge and a good number of people from Free Town. The Cherokee bride had cleaned the judge's house and the courthouse for several years and she got the judge to agree to come out to perform the legal ceremony, which occurred following the real ceremony which consisted of the little woman standing up and yelling out to the whole crowd "This here's my husband and I'm his wife from here on out! Anybody got a problem with that come see me about it and we'll git it straightened out right then and there." That settled it – nobody had any problems, and as soon as they had made their vows with the judge, everyone gathered near a cooking pit in the ground from which two pigs had been removed. They all, including the judge, ate the pigs and celebrated the marriage. Out of deference to the sensibilities of the groom no one said anything about ground coons.

About a month after the little Cherokee woman married the ex-deputy, she took him to a church in Free Town. As was the custom, she and her new husband sat at the back of the church since he was a white man. She had told the preacher about a week earlier that she was going to be there with her husband. The preacher preached about forgiveness and the love that God has for us and how Jesus wants us all to forgive each other and love each other no matter what we have done to each other in the past. At the end of the sermon the preacher made an alter call, inviting anyone to come forward if he had anything on his heart that he wished to share with the congregation. The deputy looked around for a moment and then took a step forward and then another, and by the time he got past the third or fourth row from the back, black hands at the end of each pew reached out to steady him as he anxiously moved forward on his new artificial feet. His woman walked behind him. When he reached the front he turned to the audience and looked down at the floor and simply said "I'm sorry," and he started sobbing, and his shoulders moved up and down and he kept sobbing. The singing had stopped and tears were coursing down black faces and the room was quiet except for the sobbing and the deputy kept crying as some of the men helped him stand there since he didn't have any toes to balance himself, and the Spirit of God filled the room and there was peace and healing on the mountain.

~ ~ ~

Meanwhile, long before the union of the little Cherokee woman and the legless ex-deputy sheriff, the high sheriff himself spoke several times in the weeks following the big barbeque in town about what a great pig picking that was, and how it contributed to a sense of community on the mountain, especially since they had held it right down town on the courthouse square.

For most of the summer following the courthouse barbeque there was a general sense of peace on the mountain, except in the homes of the men who had been shot. The men who had been injured in the coon hunting accidents spent the ensuing weeks and months learning to walk again. Their wives did the work that their men would have been doing had they not been so unfortunately shot in the legs. The women punished their men for this by doing absolutely nothing for them. When the women cooked they prepared only enough for themselves. They couldn't skip milking the cows because the cows would die from mastitis, so they milked them, set aside enough for themselves to drink and to make just enough butter and clabber for their own consumption, and fed the rest to the pigs. The men had no milk to drink, no clabber to mix with cornbread, and no cornbread or biscuits unless they made it themselves. When they dressed their husbands' wounds the women would press and poke and scrub in such a way that the men yelled and broke out into sweats, and the women broke out into smiles. Then they went into the fields, where their husbands should have been, and did their own sweating, while anticipating with pleasure the changing of the men's dressings in the evening. In the evening the wounds were salted as was the custom then, to kill the germs, and the women would push the salt into the hole with a finger that was slightly larger than the hole to make sure it got deep enough to do some good. The men yelled, but they used all their strength to keep from yelling loud enough for their neighbors to hear them.

These women generally had a very happy and productive summer.

Thus it was that over a year later, after what came to be known as The Trial, as if only one trial in all the history of the mountain had so distinguished itself from all the rest that it alone merited, indeed required, the use of the definite article without more, *The* Trial, and after what the judge did the day following the trial, Free Town (or as it was known to the sheriff, the Klansmen, and many others, Nigger Town) was probably the most well-armed concentration of colored people its size south of the Mason-Dixon line, or come to think of it, probably north of the Mason-Dixon line. Free Town was full of guns and ammunition and mad black folks. And all the inhabitants of Free Town considered that this was righteous because almost all the guns and ammunition had been distributed by congregations of the church in Free Town. This concentration of guns and ammunition among the coloreds would later become a source of great consternation among many on the mountain following The Trial.

THE JUDGE

The judge who presided at The Trial was my father, Judge Jonathan Wesley Steadings. And although he was our judge, by definition a man of fairly high standing in our part of the country, he took life day by day and had his ups and downs like everyone on the mountain. Some people even said you couldn't tell he was a judge when he was off the bench because he might get in a scrap just like the next man and he hung around with some of the low lifes on the mountain. In other words although his status was hifalutin, hardly anyone on the mountain considered him to be hifalutin.

One day late in the summer following the Cherokee education of the Klan, a few weeks before our local music competition, Daddy and I were outside doing some yard work and Lady, our Bassett

Hound, was hanging out with us, as dogs do. Mr. Higginbotham lived three houses down the street and he had some visitors from California who had brought a big dog with them. While we were doing the yard work, their dog came running down the street toward us and when he got to Lady he jumped on her and bit her on the neck. She yelped and started bleeding and went down but the dog kept biting her. Daddy picked up a shovel and hit the dog on the head with it, hard. It looked to me like the dog was knocked out, but in a moment he yelped and got up and when Daddy started at him again he ran back up toward Mr. Higginbotham's house with his tail between his legs yelping all the way. The California guy who owned the dog was standing outside and could see the attack from down the street, and when Daddy hit his dog the man came running down the street and rushed up to Daddy and started yelling right in his face.

Daddy just stood there looking at the man straight in the face and waited for him to finish yelling. The man stopped and stood menacingly in front of Daddy, and then Daddy said to him,

"Mister, I don't know you – never seen you before in my life, and I'm not going to say this but one time. My dog was down here in her own yard minding her own business, not bothering anybody, and your dog came running down here and picked a fight with my dog. So I took this shovel and I hit your dog in the head with it real hard." He motioned with the shovel toward the man, as if to make sure the man saw what he was talking about.

The man was getting madder.

Daddy paused for a moment.

"And now here *I* am down here in *my* own yard minding *my* own business not bothering anybody, and now *you* come running down here wanting to pick a fight with *me.*"

Daddy still had the shovel in his hand.

And that's all he said. He didn't say "I'm the local judge" or "Get off my property" or anything like that. I could see the man was startled – this was not what he had expected. I could sense him processing the moment, perceiving the parallels, still wild eyed. He looked at the shovel in Daddy's hand for a moment and then turned around and stomped off. We never saw their dog again, and the next day the visitors were gone from the Higginbotham house before we ate breakfast. A few months later the Higginbothams moved out to California and we never heard from them again. But before they moved they would say hello and act like nothing had ever happened. Later that year Lady got hit by a car and died. Daddy cried when Mama told him what happened. Daddy pulled my wagon over to where Mama had drug Lady and picked her up and put her on the wagon, and he took that same shovel and buried her at the back of our vegetable garden. My granddaughter plays with that same wagon to this day, and I still have that shovel, and it's as good as it was fifty years ago, for gardening or whatever else.

During the early evening of the night that Mama and Daddy worked until midnight moving me and J.C. to a downstairs bedroom, which was a few days after Mr. Higginbotham's California guest narrowly avoided getting knocked in the head with a shovel, we had the preacher and his wife and an older couple from church for supper.

As usual, everybody got there about an hour ahead of mealtime.

"Y'all come on in and sit a spell," Mama said, "I'll have you some ice tea out here in just a minute." Everyone went to the living room and started shootin' the breeze. This was story time, and it played out in living rooms and kitchens and around campfires all over the mountain about this time of day. This was the way news traveled from one side of the mountain to the other within hours. Most of the stories were about current events, or more particularly about what had happened to this person or that person recently. This included farms lost through foreclosure; farms sold, farms bought; births, deaths, illnesses, and other particularized troubles or victories of interest to all. Inevitably these conversations gradually became historical rather than current, reaching back into the past and tying it to the present, telling of the culture of the mountain and indeed contributing to it. This was a live, raw history of us – The Story, without which this mountain would not be *this* mountain.

And so the old man visiting us that evening told a couple of mountain stories, ones that we had all heard before but which we enjoyed every time we heard them. Many of these mountain tales were grounded in humor because we had to have it; we could not do without laughter in our lives and remain well, and so they had to be true, or mostly so, because we had to believe them if we were really to laugh, and then they were medicine for our community spirit. We rejoiced in the victories of our heroes, were gratified by the defeats of those on whom our disapproval rested and for some reason we laughed at the misfortunes and pain of those on whom we felt Justice, whether poetic or institutional, should be visited. But it seemed that our greatest delights and satisfaction ensued when we heard about or watched poetic justice in action.

This evening Daddy was in a particularly jovial mood, and when that was the case he often told a railroad story or two.

When he was in his early twenties Daddy left the mountain and worked for the railroad during the summer to earn money for college. He primarily did grunt work in the freight yards in Rocky Mount and Richmond, and he often traveled from one city to the other in a caboose.

Daddy was committed to our system of justice, but from my earliest memories I can recall him saying that justice does not reside solely in a courtroom. When he wanted to make the point that it is in the nature of human existence that we are often blessed with and should always welcome this poetic justice, Daddy delighted in telling about something that happened on one of these trips in the caboose. I heard the story many times and it was always the same in its essentials.

Daddy had been working in the yards in Rocky Mount and he was riding in the caboose of a short freight train up to Richmond where he was supposed to work in the yards up there for a few days. Two other men and the conductor were also in the caboose. The conductor was a big hairy man who made it a point to go to church wherever he was laid over for a day or two, if that was on a Wednesday night or a Sunday, but in his day-to-day activities he tended to order his subordinates around to serve his personal needs. Generally he did nothing for himself that he could get someone else to do for him.

This train moved along fairly fast on long straight stretches in rural areas, but it would slow down in more populated areas and stretches where the tracks had tight curves. There was a coal-burning stove in the caboose on which the men made their coffee and cooked their stew or whatever they were eating that day. And although the weather was hot and humid outside, the men could keep the caboose fairly cool in the summertime by opening its windows.

On this trip they were making a pot of coffee in a heavy enameled steel pot and it had just finished percolating to a rich, dark, bubbling brew. The train was going slow. There was one small booth in the caboose where the men ate two at a time, and the conductor was sitting in it facing the rear of the train; another man was sitting on the other side of the table in the booth facing the conductor. The booth was just one seat wide and was rather compact. It was a hot day but people drank coffee all day long back then.

Daddy used to say a cup of hot coffee would cool you down in the summertime. All the men were dressed in their railroad overalls, and because of the heat the conductor wasn't even wearing a shirt.

"Git up and git me a cup of coffee," the conductor said to the man facing him.

The man got up and set a mug in front of the conductor and took the pot of still boiling coffee from the stove and started pouring coffee into the conductor's mug. Just as the man began pouring the coffee the engineer suddenly slammed on the train's brakes and instantly the stream of boiling coffee moved forward from the mug into the conductor's lap and up his chest to his neck and then down inside his overalls on his bare shirtless skin.

Daddy said the conductor just as instantly lost his composure. He tried to back away from the stream of boiling coffee but there was nowhere to go because the back of the booth stopped him, so he flailed and slapped at the coffee pot and its boiling stream which caused it to spill its full measure – the whole pot of coffee – onto his chest inside his overalls. The man who was pouring the coffee lost his balance and dropped the pot into the conductor's lap. Daddy said the conductor came out the side of the booth hollering and yelling and flailing and slapping and jumping, still trying to get the scalding liquid and the searing steel pot off his front side.

At this point in the story Daddy would often digress and talk about how we all, the simplest or even the most sophisticated of us, maintain a certain public composure, and that no matter how lowly or how hifalutin or powerful a person is there is a breakpoint at which composure no longer matters. When this breakpoint is reached it is not so much that one makes a decision to abandon one's composure but rather that one enters an ontological zone where composure doesn't matter for the simple reason that there is no issue of human relations there, and thus there is no social compact requiring a certain comportment by anyone in that zone. Daddy emphasized that when one enters that zone one is in a state of existence where there are no social constraints.

The digression often included a story about an event that occurred in one of the big law firms in Knoxville where Daddy was interviewing for a job right after he completed law school. All the candidates for the position had gone through the initial interviews and were finally being interviewed by the senior partner, who had recently completed two terms as a United States Senator before returning to his old law firm in Knoxville.

The senator was receiving two young lawyers at a time and Daddy was paired with the only female in the group of candidates. Daddy said she was a knockout gorgeous young woman, always adding that she was almost as pretty as Mama. Daddy and the young lady were escorted into the senator's office and he motioned to Daddy and the young lady to have a seat in a couple of straight back chairs across from him at a small coffee table where he was seated in a nice straight back captain's chair. He had beverages brought in and Daddy and the young lady took coffee, and the senator had water. They talked a while and the senator asked each of them to tell him about their personal background. He began with the young lady and as she talked he appeared to be enthralled by her personal story. He relaxed and leaned his chair back and listened intently, occasionally asking a question. When she was concluding he asked about her matrimonial plans and she said that there was no man in her life except her father and that she intended to wait for just the right man. The senator smiled his approval and leaned back again. He was a handsome man in his fifties, rich, well bred, well groomed, well clothed, well connected, and head of one of the south's great law firms. At approximately forty-seven degrees into the lean the senator entered the zone. He instantly relinquished all concerns about his handsomeness, his wealth, his breeding, his grooming, his clothing, his connections, his national status, and even his incipient thoughts about the beautiful young lady seated across the table from him. He let out a loud grunting sound, not quite a yell, his chin jutted forward, his eyes bugged out, his mouth opened grotesquely; he first reached for non-existent handles in the air and then flailed about, moving both arms wildly in a circle, probably in an attempt to move his center of gravity forward during that terrible pause just past the forty-seven degree point and before his descent toward the floor accelerated. None of this worked. As he crashed to the floor his legs flew up and turned over the coffee table and spilled the beverages that were still on it including the pot of coffee and accompaniments, and he knocked over a floor lamp that he tried to grab on his way down. All this made a loud commotion that brought the senator's secretary and two or three others running in. The secretary helped the senator get up off the floor. He was breathing heavily, his hair was tussled, his suit was crumpled, and there was a gap where his two upper front teeth had been. He had somehow managed to spit out a partial plate and was now looking for it on the floor. Daddy and the young lady remained seated – what could they have done in a span of two to three seconds? They were both excruciatingly embarrassed for the senator and could only smile at him and his people. The senator never looked at them. The secretary glared at the two youngsters, as if they had caused this humiliating catastrophe, and walked the senator out of the room, telling him not to worry about his false teeth, that they would find them, and Daddy and the young lady got up and left. Daddy never got to complete his interview and neither of them got the job…

But back to the caboose.

The conductor yelled as the train came to a stop and all four men including the conductor climbed down out of the caboose to see what had happened. The engineer, a big, burly man, walked as fast as he could toward the rear of the train. He walked past the men and the caboose for another seventy-five yards or so and stepped down into the ditch by the tracks and bent down. He stood up and started walking back toward the men holding a huge mud turtle.

While the engineer was hustling back to where he had seen the mud turtle the conductor was grimacing and contorting from his rapidly augmenting pain, holding his groin and jumping like a young boy who had an uncontrollable need to pee. His entire front side had been scalded from his neck down, including his privates. As the engineer approached the men and the conductor saw the mud turtle and understood why the engineer had stopped the train, and precisely why he had suffered such an intensely painful scalding, which suffering was escalating moment by moment, Daddy said the conductor exclaimed to the engineer that he should never have stopped the train just to get a mud turtle, no matter how big he was. Daddy said the conductor expressed these sentiments to the engineer using a crescendoing stream of profanity and obscenities and other highly refined forms of invective. Daddy said the conductor even made references to the engineer's mother several times during his admonitions to the engineer, and even grouped the engineer and his family right in with several forms of livestock.

The other men were stunned; they had been working with the man for years and had always known him to be a rather religious man who regularly went to church no matter what town he was in. They had never heard him cuss, and they had never heard anybody take it to the level they were now experiencing even though they had both grown up on farms down in eastern North Carolina where profanity was just another dialect.

The engineer hardly seemed to hear the conductor as he walked past the men toward the front of the train with a big smile on his face, holding his turtle up for the men to see. Daddy said the conductor continued to yell at the engineer, but the engineer never turned around. He was so focused on his prize that he never realized what had happened to the conductor. When he got to his engine, he lifted the turtle up into the cab and laid it upside down on the floor and grabbed the handrail and pulled himself up into the cabin and closed the door.

Daddy said the conductor finally stopped yelling and cussing and started grimacing and contorting and moaning again, and finally just stood still, defeated. Daddy said he was almost catatonic by now and the men had to help him back into the caboose. The men could see that he was in extreme pain from the stiff wet overalls rubbing against his burns, so they helped him remove his overalls; they mopped up the coffee with one of the sheets from a bunk, and so that he would not be stark naked for the rest of the trip to Richmond they draped the other sheet from the bunk around his neck like a barber's cloth and then laid him on his back on the floor on the thin cotton mattress from the bunk; he didn't have the strength to climb into the elevated bunk, and he wouldn't let the men lift him up there.

The other men told Daddy to flag the engineer that all were aboard and the train could start moving again. Daddy looked around the caboose but he couldn't find the conductor's flag so he used the conductor's overalls, waving them up and down outside the caboose. The engineer apparently understood the signal because the train began to move forward. Daddy saw the conductor watching him use his overalls to signal the engineer. When their eyes met the conductor looked away in a daze.

A couple of hours later they pulled into Richmond. The conductor had moaned and groaned the whole way. When the train backed into its offloading spur and stopped, the men helped the conductor down out of the caboose and all three of them walked with him to the boarding house where they stayed when they were working the yards in Richmond, two blocks from the rail yard. Daddy said there were lots of people who were out and about, and they stared at the conductor as he slowly moved down the sidewalk with the bed sheet draped around him, which was highly unusual on a public sidewalk even down by the rail yard, but the conductor didn't seem to be aware of this because he was still in a daze, barely able to put one foot in front of the other. One of the men walked in step behind the conductor holding the sheet together so that the other people could not see the conductor's bare backside. Daddy was carrying his overalls and people also stared at the overalls and at Daddy. Daddy said it only later occurred to him that some of the people staring at the overalls surely must have been wondering if the conductor had experienced some sort of bowel accident, but nobody asked. They just stopped and stared; this was probably a first for all of these people.

The men eventually got the conductor up the front steps of the boarding house and to his room and into his bed. Every time he made the slightest move he moaned. The other men left and went out onto the front porch to sit and smoke while they waited for supper.

Daddy stayed in the room with the conductor and around dark, without thinking, Daddy asked him if he would like a cup of coffee. Daddy said the conductor gasped and started shaking and his eyes went wild for an instant and then he settled and stared straight ahead. Daddy said at that point he realized he probably shouldn't say anything about coffee for a while, at least not within hearing of the conductor.

The lady who ran the boarding house knocked on the door.

"It's me. Can I come in?

"Come on in."

She stepped in and stared at the conductor. He glanced at her and then looked away. He had been staying here in her boarding house for years. She had left middle Tennessee over twenty years before when she married a soldier boy from Richmond. He had got shot dead in a bar fight a few years back and she took the ten thousand dollars insurance proceeds and bought the boarding house.

"You'uns okay? I seen you'uns comin' up the steps an' him awearin' a bed sheet. Why wuz you wearing a bed sheet right out in broad daylight?"

Without waiting for an answer she looked at Daddy, "Why wuz you carrying his overalls? He ditn' soil hisself did he?"

"Ma'am?"

"Soil hisself – mess in his pants. He didn't mess in his pants did he?" She studied the conductor, looking him up and down. The conductor looked at her wild-eyed and quickly looked away, staring at the ceiling and breathing heavily.

"Yes ma'am, we're all okay except for him. Naw, I don't think he messed in his pants, but it's possible – I hadn't thought about that." Daddy glanced at the overalls and looked at his hands front and back, and then raised them to his nose. "He got burnt on the train comin' up here. He got scalded by a whole pot of live boilin' coffee. The whole pot poured right down the front of'im inside his overalls, and he didn't even have a shirt on or any undershorts."

The conductor glanced wildly at Daddy and breathed even more heavily.

"You shoulda seen it. It was horrible, him kickin' and screamin' and flailin' and slappin' around trying to beat the hot coffee off of'im."

Daddy looked at his hands again. "You know, come to think of it, he may have had an accident during all that jumping around and being scalded." Daddy didn't mention the turtle or the cussing.

The landlady stood with her mouth open staring at the conductor; she appeared to be trying to imagine the action in the caboose. The conductor glanced at Daddy again and then looked back at the ceiling, still breathing heavily.

"Well let me know if I can do anything for'im. You reckon he needs to go to the toilet?"

She studied him. He stared at the wall beyond the foot of his bed.

"Yon't me to bring you a chamber pot in here? You need to make water?" She spoke louder to him than she had been speaking to Daddy, perhaps thinking that the scalding had affected his hearing.

The conductor grimaced as he shifted slightly. He was still breathing heavily. "I don't believe I'd be able to make water right now even if I needed to," he gasped. "I don't know if I'll ever be able to make normal water again. I'd appreciate it if y'all would just leave me alone now and let me git some rest."

"You reckon we ought to call the doctor?"

"Naw, I ain't goin' to no doctor."

"Yon't me to git you one to come here?"

"I'm tellin ya, I just need to be left alone now so I can git some rest."

"You want your supper? Everbody else is already in there eatin'."

He didn't answer. He stared straight ahead.

"I'm comin'," Daddy said, "I'm hungry. That food smells good!"

Daddy started across the hall into the dining room, leaving the bedroom door open so he could hear the conductor call him if need be, and stopped in the middle of the hall. He looked down at his hands front and back and instead of going on into the dining room he turned and walked down the hall to the bathroom and gave his hands a thorough scrubbing with a chunk of lye soap. He then joined several other men at the dining room table, where there were bowls of fried chicken and vegetables of all sorts and hushpuppies and biscuits and mashed potatoes and gravy, and although the other two men had probably already briefly recounted the events of that day, Daddy told these men a moment by moment account of what had happened, recounting in precise detail the conductor's encounter with the boiling liquid and his reaction to it as he was being scalded. The men began to chuckle as they imagined that scene, but when Daddy got to the part about the mud turtle and the cussing they started howling, and when he finally described the scene of the conductor walking through town naked as a jay bird except for the bed sheet wrapped around him, and the one man walking in step behind him holding the sheet closed, and the crowds gathering and staring at him, they couldn't talk or eat they were laughing so hard.

After a few minutes the landlady came to the dining room door that was just across the hall from the conductor's bedroom door, which was still open, and told the men to calm down for a minute – she had some good news for them. Being the southern boys that they were, the men settled down and politely obeyed, turning their attention to her.

"Y'all's engineer just brought me a big mud turtle with his head cut off and I'm gittin ready to dress it now and I'm gonna cook y'all some turtle soup for tomorrow night!"

The men looked at each other and yelled their approval – what hardworking southern man didn't love turtle soup? And at that moment from the conductor's bedroom came a loud sobbing wail and then the sound of something crashing to the floor. The landlady hurried into his room and found the conductor still in bed, still partially covered, panting and sweating heavily. The lamp and his bedside table lay on the floor.

"What's wrong?" She stared at his groin area, which was still covered by the sheet. "You hurtin' from not being able to pass water?"

"You gonna cook that turtle in the kitchen?"

"Where else would I cook a turtle?"

"I gotta get outta here before you start cooking that turtle!"

"What for? You cain't even move. You cain't make water and you cain't walk and no telling what else you cain't do! What you got against that turtle?"

"Please don't cook that turtle tomorrow. I just need a few days to get well."

"I cain't do that. That'd be a waste of a whole lot of good turtle meat that'd go bad – it won't keep in the ice box. What you got against turtle soup now? You've eat it before rightchere in this house and loved it."

"Would you throw it away for an extra month's rent? I just don't believe I can stand the smell of that turtle cooking in the morning."

"I cain't do that. It's not my turtle to throw away. It belongs to y'all's engineer and he wants me to cook it. Besides, I'll bring you a bowl of it in here and you can eat it rightchere in this room. You won't have to go in yonder to eat. It'll give you some strength and perk you right up and that's what you need. I'll take care of ya." She kept glancing at his groin area. The sheet covered him to a couple of inches below his belly button, and above that she could see red raw flesh with skin peeling away.

"What happened to this lamp and this bedside table?"

The conductor was panting more heavily now. He looked at her and then quickly back at the ceiling.

He was almost breathless. She stooped and lifted the table and put the lamp back in place.

"I'm gonna bring you that chamber pot in here when I finish cleaning that turtle. You ain't fit to even walk down the hall to the toilet. Now you just settle down and rest. I'll bring you some of that turtle soup tomorrow evenin' and you'll be better before you know it! I bet you anything that just smellin' it cookin' all day'll make you feel better. I'm gonna soak the meat in salt water with a little vinegar in it all night to take the stink out of it 'fore I start cooking it."

He gagged.

"I promise I'll bring you the first bowl of it!"

He gasped and closed his eyes.

"Now I got to get out there and dress'im 'fore dark. You need anything else other'n the chamber pot? I've even got a little bed pot for passing water in bed that I'll bring ya. Yont it now?"

He opened his eyes and glanced at her and then turned away and stared at the wall. She left the room. He closed his eyes and tried to sleep.

In a few minutes he could hear the sound of the hatchet coming from the back yard as she split the turtle's shell, chop, chop, chop. The men had finished eating and were back on the front porch smoking. The whacking of the hatchet became louder. Off in the distance a rooster crowed. He opened his eyes and the room was spinning... He sensed it before it started... He tried to rise but his legs wouldn't move... He felt the trickle and then the flow began... He yelled for the bed pot.

This was usually the end of the story because Daddy would be laughing so hard that he couldn't talk any more. Such was the case this evening; the whole crowd was in stitches when Mama stuck her head in the door. "Y'all come on in – supper's ready."

We all got up and went to the supper table. And even though the preacher was there, and the older gentleman from our church, Daddy said the mealtime prayer, after which we all dug in and the talking resumed.

During the meal the conversation got around to sports and Daddy remarked to the preacher that he looked very athletic and fit.

~   ~   ~

"Thanks, Jon. Nellie and I get together about three times a week at the Community Center to exercise with some other couples from church."

"Well, whatever you're doing it sure seems to be working. You look great."

"We do calisthenics and some weight lifting. We work out as a group so we can encourage each other and keep up the pace. I think that really helps us stay with it."

My brother J.C. piped up and said, "Mama and Daddy work out about three times a week right here at the house. I can hear'em doing calisthenics in their bedroom after Jackson and I go to bed. And Mama always encourages Daddy, too." The idiot had never used the word calisthenics in his life.

During those years Mama and Daddy slept upstairs at the end of the hall and my brother and I slept in a room next to theirs. Their bedroom door was always closed at night and of course we were not allowed to open it without their permission. There were clothes closets between the rooms but we could still hear them talking and snoring in their room. Both of them snored, and both denied it.

My brother was two years younger than me and during those years I was convinced that he was an idiot (today he's our governor). He was born Jonathan Charles Steadings, but we called him J.C. He was named after Daddy except they didn't have the same middle name. He didn't like to be called Charles and we couldn't call him Jon or Jonathan because it would get too confusing around the house, so we all settled on J.C. and that was fine by him.

"What do you mean I encourage Daddy?" Mama asked J.C. She looked puzzled.

"Because I can hear you telling Daddy, 'Don't stop, Don't stop,' and ya'll keep on doing calisthenics for awhile. I can hear ya." J.C. was beaming – obviously proud of Mama and Daddy, and of his new word.

Silence.

After a few moments a rooster crowed way off in the distance, gently piercing the night with his bedtime crowing.

The sound of the crickets outside became almost deafening…

A dog barked somewhere.

J.C. and I looked around at everybody. Nobody was looking at anybody. Nobody was saying anything.

Daddy looked intently at the bowl of mashed potatoes.

The preacher and his wife looked at their plates silently; she shot a quick glance at the radiators and he studied the chandelier for a moment.

The older couple looked through the window at the beautiful street lights outside that were illuminating our street and sidewalk.

Mama looked like she was taking the flu. I'd never seen it come on that fast.

I watched Daddy as he looked harder at the bowl of mashed potatoes and pursed his lips.

After two or three minutes of absolute silence, the older man spoke up and told J.C. how it was good for us to keep on exercising all our lives because that's what keeps us in good shape. That and eating good meals like this and spending time together and encouraging one another. He was an elder at our church and had baptized me in the creek the year before.

"I still love to exercise regularly, J.C., yessiree, I shore do. But I cain't do calisthenics quite as much as I used to. Back in my day I'd sometimes do calisthenics two or three times a day."

Mama made a high-pitched sound and jumped up and rushed into the kitchen.

J.C. was still beaming. It was rare that adults addressed him with this degree of approbation.

The old man's wife glared at him and made a snorting sound. "That's been awhile," she grunted, as she jumped up and followed Mama into the kitchen.

By now practically comatose, Daddy continued to study the mashed potatoes, and the preacher and his wife resumed feeding and reloading as needed to keep a supply on their plates.

"Jon, would you please pass the mashed potatoes?" the old man asked merrily.

Daddy reached for the bowl of mashed potatoes in slow motion and handed it to him without looking at him or at anybody else at the table and the old gentleman thereupon spooned himself a massive serving of them and dug in.

"Man these mashed potatoes are good! I flat out believe they're the best I've ever eat."

When Mama and the elder's wife returned to the table with dessert and coffee it looked like they were both taking the flu, what with their red eyes and general demeanor. Nobody except the old man ate much dessert, which was unusual in this house, and after a few minutes of nobody looking at each other while they slurped their coffee, the guests left. As they were leaving, the old man motioned for J.C. to come over and give him a hug, which left J.C. almost beside himself. I don't believe I have ever seen J.C. as happy as he was that night.

I watched the old man walk with his wife to their car, whistling all the way, and when they got to the car, he jumped in front of his wife and opened her door for her and bowed with a sweep of his arm, motioning for her to enter.

After everybody left, Mama and Daddy moved J.C. and me to the first floor bedroom next to Daddy's study at the other end of the house. They completely switched the contents of the two bedrooms that night. It took us until almost midnight. J.C. and I had never stayed up that late except when we went to see Daddy's lawyer friend in Chicago and when we went down to New Orleans on vacation where we usually stayed with another one of Daddy's law school friends who was a state senator. J.C. and I kept asking what the big hurry was, but they just kept moving. Afterwards, when J.C. and I were in bed in our new room, I heard Mama crying and laughing at the same time and making shrieking noises way up in her bedroom at the other end of the house before I fell asleep. I had never heard this combination before. I didn't hear Daddy at all.

A Town Hall

Our place was like many others in town, except a little larger than most, although certainly not the largest. We had about three acres and we were seven blocks from the courthouse square. Some people at the edge of town had plots of fifteen or twenty acres. We had chickens and always three or four pigs, and every year Daddy bought a young steer and put it on our pasture which was a little over an acre. Like everybody in town that I ever saw, we had a garden that gave us all the vegetables that we could possibly eat throughout the year, and then some. We were constantly giving away vegetables to people who came by but I don't know what they did with them because I'm sure they had gardens too – everybody in town did. Maybe they fed them to their pigs. We certainly did. And we had a little corn field, about a half acre, which with garden scraps and kitchen slops, including our dishwater, fed our hogs right up to hog killing in November or December every year. Mama used lye soap for washing the dishes, and the hog swill that we made with it wormed the hogs. They loved it, and we had healthy hogs.

The old aristocratic houses were mostly within a block or two of the square and from there on out to the edge of town were generally smaller houses on progressively larger plots of land; occasionally some of the younger generation who had made or come into money would build a big house out toward the edge of town on a big piece of land and would run their various enterprises from there. Most had domestic servants who resided in small but comfortable houses on the estate.

On the other side of the square from the old money, down toward the railroad, lived most of the white people in our town. Just beyond the railroad was a narrow band of shacks occupied by the less fortunate whites among us, and just beyond them were situated the first small Negro holdings, the beginning of Free Town. A progression of affluence similar to the white side of town could be observed as one traveled away from the railroad tracks through Free Town toward its outer edge. But almost without exception all these holdings, large and small, had one thing in common: they all produced food. Every one of them had a garden beside the house or behind the house, or both; and most of them had some form of livestock, even if it was only a dozen or so hens, and maybe a milk goat or a hutch of rabbits. Three does and a buck could easily provide a family with three hundred pounds of rabbit meat a year.

Occasionally people would move to the mountain from up north, or from down south where they had moved to escape the cold weather and found it too hot down there. One evening a couple of these outsiders, a woman and her husband, came to one of our monthly city council meetings, which were always well attended by many of our townsmen, and during the public statements part of the meeting asked to be heard on a matter they said they were very concerned about. The lady read from a prepared statement that she had written out.

"Council Members, my husband and I want to bring something to your attention that has been troubling us since we moved to this town.

"We moved down here three years ago. In the town where we lived before moving here it was illegal to keep livestock on your property if it was inside the city limits. The health department had done some studies of the dangers of keeping livestock in populated areas, especially chickens and hogs.

"My husband and I believe the time has come for this town to pass an ordinance prohibiting the keeping of any kind of livestock within the city limits, for the same reasons that many cities have passed such ordinances, namely the public health. We also believe the town would smell a lot cleaner without livestock in everybody's back yard, and people wouldn't be bothered by the incessant crowing of roosters. They crow throughout the day and night here, and the whole town has a very unpleasant smell. Thank you."

The mayor thanked the lady and asked if there was any discussion from the council or if any of the council members had any questions. The council members sat there and looked at the lady. The mayor sat there and looked at the lady. The lady stood at the podium and looked at the council and the mayor. The mayor waited, still looking at the lady. For a full two minutes nobody said anything. Somebody coughed. The lady looked uncomfortable. Two minutes is a long, long time when everybody in the room is staring at you. Finally the mayor looked at the members to his right and his left and then he spoke.

"Ma'am, there's not a snowball's chance in hell that this council will ever pass such an ordinance. We've just come through what a lot of folks call the worst depression this country's ever seen, but nobody in this town or on this mountain starved. They didn't even get really hungry. There was very little money around, but our babies still got fat. In fact, every family in town had meat on the table when they wanted it. They had vegetables galore and those vegetables grew so plentifully because the folks here in town used their cow manure and their hog manure and their chicken and rabbit manure to fertilize their gardens. Our people had milk and clabber and cream and butter. They had fresh eggs every day of the year. Some people may think manure stinks, but here on the mountain we think it is one of the sweetest fragrances in the world. And I doubt that you could find a single person here in town that really hears the roosters crowing, much less being bothered by'em. In fact they'd probably miss the crowing if we didn't have'em.

"We're mighty proud to have ya'll as neighbors – we always try to make outsiders feel welcome here – and we certainly don't expect you and your husband to bother with keeping any livestock in your backyard, but we won't be telling our people that they can't keep a cow and some pigs and some chickens on their little places here in town. And if you need any country cured ham or bacon or stuffed sausage or eggs, there's plenty of folks here in town that will be glad to sell you some. Just this morning my wife was talking about what in the world we're gonna do with all these extra eggs we've got. If you and your husband need some just drop by the house and she'll fix you right up.

"As always, Ma'am, you're welcome to write up a petition and have two hundred voters sign it to force us to vote on an ordinance, but I am pretty sure that none of these councilmen is gonna do it by bringing a motion before the council. And frankly I doubt that you could find ten people in this town that would sign a petition. Again we want to thank you Ma'am, for participating in our democratic process here on the mountain, and you come speak to us any time you take a notion to."

Again there was silence in the room. And then everybody in the audience started clapping. If the lady was uncomfortable during the silence that preceded this speech, she was now downright beaten. She and her husband walked out of the council room and to my knowledge never returned. A couple of years later they moved somewhere and nobody on the mountain ever heard from them or missed them. People in town still have their pigs and cows and chickens, and until he died Daddy fattened a steer every year on his little one acre pasture.

The Rose and the Rattler

One early summer morning when the dew was still on the roses, and the morning sun made the dew droplets sparkle like tiny diamonds, Mama worked in her flower beds outside. She loved to see dew on the roses and to smell them at that time of day. She was putting down some mulch under a patch of roses that she had in the side yard. As she reached under a bush to push some mulch around to even it out, she heard what sounded like a cricket and felt a thump and a sharp sting on her forearm, about three or four inches below her elbow. Startled, she yelped and looked closely under the bush and saw a timber rattler ready to strike again. She jumped back and yelled for me and rushed toward the front porch. J.C. and I were playing on the other side of the house and I could tell something was wrong by the way Mama yelled for me.

She called again and I got to the front porch about the same time she did.

"I just got snake bit!" she yelled.

"Where?"

"Right here on my arm. Go call Daddy and tell'im to come get me, right now!"

I ran to the phone and called Daddy's office and told his secretary what had happened and hung up. I ran back to Mama and she was already tying a headscarf around her arm just below her elbow using her good arm and her teeth.

"Finish tying this knot here," she said, "and then stick these shears through it and start twisting. I'll tell you when to stop."

I tied the knot and started twisting.

She grimaced. "That's tight enough. Daddy ought to be here in a minute." She was breathing heavily.

A couple of minutes later Daddy sped into the driveway and jumped out of the car and reached out and took Mama's hand.

"That there's a real snake bite right there," he said excitedly. "Let's get you in the car right now!"

Daddy helped Mama get in the front and I jumped in the back seat and we headed for the hospital.

When we pulled up to the emergency entrance, Dr. Allison was the only doctor at the hospital and we could see him down the hall in the colored people's area.

"We don't have a doctor here, but I can get one here in about ten minutes," said the duty nurse.

"What do you think he is?" Daddy asked, pointing to Dr. Allison.

"But he's a Negro, Judge!"

Daddy just ignored her and took Mama by the arm and walked up to Dr. Allison and told him that Mama had just been bitten by a rattler. Dr. Allison helped Mama take a seat. He examined the wound and the tourniquet.

"We'll leave that tourniquet as it is for just a moment until I inject a serum to start counteracting the venom."

A nurse had already fetched the serum and a syringe and needle. Dr. Allison filled the syringe and gently administered the injection as Mama sat quietly and watched.

"You're going to be a sick lady for a couple of days and there'll be serious swelling and pain so I'd recommend that you stay here at least until tomorrow so we can keep you under observation and keep you as comfortable as possible."

He loosened the tourniquet and within a few minutes she said she was feeling nauseous.

"I'll go ahead and admit you and we'll get you a room over on the other side. Who's your doctor?"

Daddy looked at Mama and she nodded. "You are!" snapped Daddy, "and Molly'll take a room over in this section since this is where you are." Dr. Allison looked thoughtfully at both of them.

"Are you sure about this? This will be a first, and you know there will be consequences."

Mama and Daddy looked at each other again.

"We're sure," said Daddy.

The doctor called a colored nurse who arrived with a wheelchair. "Let's just ease you right down in this chair and we'll get you right into a bed," she said. She smiled at Mama and placed her black hand on Mama's hand. "We're gonna take good care of you sweetheart."

Mama smiled back at her. "I know you will." And down the hall they went. Thus occurred what was probably one of the first instances of racial activism on the mountain. Because she was so sick Mama ended up spending three days there under Dr. Allison's care, and for weeks afterward the mountain was abuzz with talk about how the judge of all people had put his wife in the nigger section of the hospital and had used the nigger doctor to treat her. As far as I could tell, this never seemed to bother either Daddy or Mama. In fact, if anything, they seemed to enjoy it.

As for myself, I've often thought about the contrast between that beautiful rose and that deadly serpent beneath it, and how that timber rattler's bite that morning figured in a series of events that would eventually change the whole mountain.

Keynote Sermon
by the Archbishop
of Appalachia

T housands of preachers, teachers, pastors, bishops, elders, deacons, and overseers had gathered in the southern highlands for an annual convention. There were souls there from high church and from low church and from no church. For three days there were talks and sermons and panel discussions and seminars about organizational tactics and strategies and church growth and ecclesiastical architecture and fundraising and partnering with government and non-governmental organizations and fundraising and youth programs and fundraising and integrating youth into the broader community and fundraising. The organizers had asked Archie, the self-appointed archbishop of Appalachia, to deliver the closing sermon, hoping that he would bring validation and affirmation to their agenda. He was after all a highly educated man and the most popular preacher in Appalachia among the low church and no church folks. Archie stepped up to the lectern. The audience was hushed; about three thousand people listened:

ekklesia

—Within each of us there is a stirring that is set in motion by a singular call from the heart of God. It comes to all of us, this call, but in most of us the stirring wanes and like embers that have glowed for a moment and then died, the sound of the call fades and the stirring ceases. But again and again the Creator calls; He never stops, and in a few the stirring is augmented and quickened by the content of the call and the delicacies of the feast that these few perceive.

Abraham our forebear heard this call and felt this stirring, and he tasted these delicacies because he broke his bonds and left his home and came to the feast. And like him others in the flow of time have heard the call and felt the stirring and have turned toward the Source and have cried Abba! and they have feasted.

The call endures. He came to us and lived among us and we killed him. But he rose and forgave us, and Abba now reaches out to gather us and to draw us into the great eternal assembly, where we feast and where our souls are safe and protected as we march into eternity.

And Abba says I AM, come to me.

And we say Abba, break these chains!

And Abba says come!

And we say Abba, help us!

And Abba says come!

And we say Abba, save us!

And Abba says come to me!

And we say Abba! Abba!

—What if the church, the ekklesia, really proclaimed the good news of the kingdom of God? What would the message be? What if the church told the whole truth? What if we spoke to our young people of the deceitfulness of wealth and told them that life does not consist in an abundance of possessions? What if we taught them the joy of simplicity and the satisfaction of enough? What if we spoke of the peace and rest that come from exhaustive service to others? What if the church taught its leaders that their flock is much greater than individual assemblies? What if we prayed again and again that we might see the church as Jesus sees it? What if we opened the eyes of our soul and saw the Paraclete at work?

I taught a class at church several years ago called Christians, Jack Mackerel, and Eternal Life. It was a good class. A few years later I taught it again. It was a good class again. If you teach the truth about Christians, Jack Mackerel, and Eternal Life it will be a good class even again. The truth of simplicity and of enough never changes. Many leaders of the church have forgotten this.

Soon I would like to be in a class called Rice and Beans, Jesus, and the Great Assembly. Will you help me teach it?

And another called Puppy Breath. I love puppy breath. Have you ever smelled puppy breath? A class in the assembly of the saints called Puppy Breath? Yes, we could do it. No, I have not lost my mind. Do you know who created puppy breath?

And another about moonrise. One time I saw the movement of a full moon as it rose on the horizon. I saw the moon moving! But here's the catch: I had to stop and be still and look to see that movement. I need a class on stopping and being still.

And rest. A class on rest. Yes, that would be holy.

Tomorrow. What would we say to our young people if we taught a class about tomorrow?

A class about angels and exquisite experiences in which God draws us to him. A wild owl perched on my finger for close to an hour one time. He had got stuck in my barn and I had rescued him. He was flapping about trying to get out through a glass window. I reached up and held out my finger and he stepped onto it. I walked the hundred yards or so to the house and he stayed there all the way perched on my finger. He could have left me at any time. For an hour or so he and I marveled at each other as we moved about the house and the porch, and finally I stood on the porch and lifted my hand and he flew away. I drew closer to God with that owl on my finger. That happened. Angels.

Experiences of the simple. I remember one such experience when with just a handful of twigs I made a cup of tea in the fireplace in an old farmhouse. The house had no electricity and no running water and I had been living there for several months, cooking my meals in the fireplace or over a fire outside. I filled a metal cup with water, set it on three small rocks, and put the twigs under the cup and lit them. I was doing an experiment in simplicity and frankly I doubted that the tiny handful of twigs, less than half the volume of the water in the cup, would be enough to heat the water to a boil, but it was! I have never forgotten the amazement and the satisfaction that I experienced in that moment of simplicity and enough. Enough.

Back to dogs. A sweet, humble dog came to live with me one day. She showed up at my place with a leaf in her mouth. I had never seen her before. She was a black, short haired, medium size dog, and every single time she approached a human being, without fail, she picked up a leaf and brought it as an offering. I named her Leafer. We loved each other. One day I found her lying dead in a field in front of my house. She had a leaf in her mouth. Her final offering. Angels. One day I hope to learn and to teach about angels. I have a long way to go.

Yes, that stirring is there. It is there, moving. With the ears of our soul, if we listen, we hear that call from the heart of God. The feast is spread. The Paraclete serves delicacies that are unnamable. Abba! Abba!

There was a complete hush in the assembly. Archie looked at his people. He had intended to stop here. Short and sweet! But he had more to say.

I know I'm a strange sort of fellow, but I am a disciple of Jesus and I have committed myself to a life of service and prayer. I pray for the entire church in Appalachia and I have devoted my life and my thinking and my service to this region. My view is that God has given me spiritual responsibilities for this great flock; Appalachia is my flock not because I have been appointed by any earthly ecclesiastical institution, but because I have decided to focus my prayer and spiritual life on this region, as a follower of the teachings of Jesus. The ekklesia passage above is a transcript of a sermon that one of our preachers presented to a high church congregation, at their invitation, and their leaders were offended by it. They were offended! They came to me and asked me to chastise the man, and gave me a printed transcript of his sermon, which I have just shared with you. I told them I am not about to quench the Spirit, and that they would do well to listen to this sermon and learn from it. So they determined to have me dismissed, but they could not do it because nobody hired me to start with; I answer to God. If I'm not hired, I can't be fired. No matter what they do with or to me, they cannot keep me from serving you. I live to serve you. And no earthly institution can take that away from us. That is freedom.

For several years one of my core prayers has been that I might see the church, the ekklesia, as Jesus sees it. As most of you, I come from a deep-rooted church tradition which is fundamentally exclusionary in that we denied affiliation, association, or what many called fellowship, to those who did not share our very precise doctrinal perceptions and behavioral regulations. Any mention of, or even the vaguest allusion to, the Holy Spirit, was likely to get one ostracized, or at the very least asked to consider moving their membership to avoid conflict in the local congregation. The thinking was that it should be clear to anyone who thought about the matter that the activities of the Holy Spirit in human affairs had ceased upon the completion of the biblical canon, whatever and whenever that was, and from that time forward God's Holy Spirit acted only through the biblical message. That is the tradition from which my walk with Christ developed. I am grateful for much of that tradition because it gave me a good foundation in biblical learning and taught me to appreciate the cohesion of local assemblies, both of which remain important tenets of our faith. We refer to our assembly as family, and that is what it is and should be. We take care of each other. We support each other. When we sin — an area in which I have developed extensive personal experience — we reach out our hands and pull each other back. We are family. But I thank God that he has put a hook in my nose and has led me out of this false doctrine of the death of the Holy Spirit. The Comforter, the Paraclete, the Advocate, the Helper, whatever we want to call him, is alive and well, and all we have to do to perceive him and his activities is to listen with the ears of our soul and see with the eyes of our heart. Once we do this we have these exquisite encounters and we draw closer to our Lord through them. He teaches us in them, and we rub shoulders with him, and we sense unspeakable glory. Abba teaches us through jack mackerel and rice and beans, and moonrises, and owls perched on our finger and staring at us, and the simplicity of a tiny fire to make a cup of tea, and a dog with a leaf in her mouth as she crosses over into eternity. He does this for us. The feast is there. The Paraclete is our server; and he is not dead. Our God is not dead. This is the truth and this truth sets us free if we accept it. If we are not moved by these encounters we are dead.

I believe that Jesus has answered my prayer about seeing the church the way he sees it, but I cannot fully articulate this. I doubt that anyone can if we are honest with ourselves. He said that the kingdom of God is not something that we can point to and say There it is. He has answered my prayer by helping me refrain from saying There it is. He has helped me understand that the kingdom, and by extension the church, the ekklesia, is within us, or among us. He has helped me to see that I don't need to set up boundaries and parameters and say That defines the church. He has helped me understand that he defines the church; I just follow him. He is the sovereign.

I believe that elders, bishops, overseers, who share these views will see their flock as more than the aggregate of the members in their local assemblies. It is clear that the early church elders saw themselves as shepherds of a broad flock in a designated place. Thus we have references to the 'elders in Ephesus,' the 'elders in Jerusalem,' 'elders in every town,' etc. It is true that Acts 14.23 refers to elders in every church, but to say that this means that elders are limited to local groups, what we usually call congregations, begs the question. It appears to me that 'every church' meant the ekklesia, the broader assembly, in every town. 'Every church' could have sub-assemblies, groups meeting in different homes, or in different public or private places, such as in Jerusalem for example, but 'the church in Jerusalem' certainly meant the aggregate of all these sub-assemblies.

I recognize that this view of the flock is not congruent with much of our general tradition, but it is biblical. Tradition does not trump truth. And for this reason I pray for elders or shepherds who see the flock differently than our general tradition. I pray for elders who see their flock as the church in places, and who will deal with the fallout resulting from this view however they must with the help of the Holy Spirit. This is a spiritual matter, and the Spirit will guide and nurture the shepherds of the flock wherever they are, and no matter what barriers Satan throws up, which he is certain to do.

Blessings upon all of you. Leave here knowing that we are not an institution. Remember, the Master himself said 'You can't point to it and say There it is.' There is nothing complicated about it. Nobody can ever take you away from this family.

Peace. I'm off to eat with some friends at a little place just on the other side of the railroad tracks. They specialize in greens and beans, and a bowl of rice. That's what I'm having. I love'em!

Archie smiled and waved as he left the lectern. The applause and the boos were thunderous.

The Boarding House

Vincent Bossard, known to everyone as Vinny, lived at the boarding house for three reasons: it was near downtown, Miss Sophie's food was superb, and she let him take a bath every day if he wanted to. He didn't work at a public job because he didn't have to. Every month he received a government pension that gave him enough money to pay Miss Sophie for room and board, which was essentially all he needed, and after he had paid that he still had twice that much money left over to spend or save. He saved a lot more than he spent. He was able to do this because he wore a suit of clothes for years, and what else was there to spend anything on? Miss Sophie washed and ironed for him for an extra three dollars a month, so after that anything that he spent his money on, he considered to be for luxury.

Vinny smoked five cigars every day the sun rose except on Sunday. But even this didn't cost him anything because a tobacco company in Durham sent him three boxes of cigars every month because they said they especially appreciated what he had done for the country. Each box had fifty cigars in it, so he received one hundred and fifty cigars every month, which was more than enough for him given the fact that he cut back to only three or four cigars on Sundays.

Vinny smoked fewer cigars on Sundays because he didn't smoke during church and Sunday School, but he actually smoked more tobacco on Sundays than on the other days. He did it this way: when he got down toward the end of each cigar that he smoked during the day, he took out his pocket knife, opened a blade, and stuck it into the cigar as close to the mouth end as possible. He was thereby able to hold the cigar with his blade and smoke it down to a smaller stub than if he held it with his fingers toward the end of the smoke because his fingers started getting burned when the cigar got down to about an inch not counting the ash. By using this method of completing his smoke, Vinny ended up with a much smaller stub than he would have otherwise. But even here Vinny practiced his innate frugality, for he did not discard this stub by throwing it onto the courthouse lawn, or even putting it in one of the nearby ash trays. Instead, after he had allowed the cigar to burn out, he carefully rubbed the ash off the end and placed it in a small goat hide leather pouch that he had acquired in Cuba in 1899 after the war. On Sundays, he took these accumulated stubs and chopped them into tobacco flakes and smoked this tobacco in his pipe. Uncle Vinny was both a cigar smoker and a pipe smoker, but all in all he preferred his cigars — he just didn't want to be wasteful. When someone once asked him if this chopped tobacco from the ends of the cigars didn't taste nasty, he said No, no man — these cigars are like life — they get better toward the end.

What Vinny had done for his country that the tobacco company in Durham especially appreciated was he left the lower part of his leg in Cuba in 1899. When the major army evacuated Cuba that year after they had won the war, the United States left the black Ninth Infantry Regiment there to support the occupation. They did this because seventy-five percent of the white soldiers got the fever while they were there, but the blacks seemed to be immune to it for the most part; by the time they left only 73 of the Ninth's 984 soldiers had got the fever.

But Vinny hadn't got his leg shot off in a real battle. He lost it when he was ordered to chase down one of his own colleagues who had moved into a house of ill repute in downtown Havana. He had gone after the errant soldier, who was actually a white man who declined to evacuate with the rest of the force because he preferred his current living conditions over those that he knew he would experience if he returned to his daddy's farm in Alabama. After inquiring at the house of ill repute about the errant soldier, Vinny was directed to a small town several miles outside Havana where someone told him the soldier was setting up a new business. Vinny got to the town and someone alerted the soldier that a man in uniform was looking for him so he started running out of town. Vinny chased him and the soldier led him through a swamp where Vinny got snake bit right at his knee. He nevertheless continued and caught up with the soldier, who ended up having to tote Vinny back to town because by the time Vinny had finally caught up with him he, Vinny, had become so sick he could hardly move. Notwithstanding his current circumstances, this soldier was still a good man — he was just committed to ameliorating his living conditions and he believed that Havana and its environs constituted a prime location for doing that. He was scheduled to be honorably discharged from the army as soon as he set foot on American soil anyway. And he couldn't let a comrade in arms just die without helping him, if help him he could.

The soldier enlisted the services of a mule wagon and driver and transported Vinny back to Havana and dropped him off at the first hospital that he came to. The medicos saved Vinny's life but not his leg. They cut it off just above the knee, mended the stump, and took him to his bivouac as soon as he was well enough to be moved there. The soldier that Vinny had been chasing stayed in Havana and became a very successful businessman. The army put into his records that he had died in a swamp from the fever. As the years passed, the character of his investments evolved, becoming more conventional, and in 1919 he cashed in and returned to Alabama, where he bought three farms adjoining his daddy's place, hired a farm manager to oversee the three tenant farmers who ran the farms, and placed his daddy in charge of the whole operation at a salary that was more than five times what he had ever made in a year of farming. After he got his daddy settled in and established as a serious farm operator, the former soldier moved to Durham and started a tobacco importing business, specializing in Caribbean, especially Cuban, cigars.

Vinny convalesced in Havana for three months after losing his leg, and finally made it back to New Orleans where he had grown up as Vincent Bossard among many siblings and cousins and other distant relatives who had paid him very little mind until he returned with his disabled veteran's pension. This income was sufficient to sustain him, but because of the love visited upon him by so many of his relatives, Vinny was penniless by the middle of every month. So after the middle of the month he hobbled down to the Quarter with his crutches and harmonica — known as a harp by everybody south of the Mason-Dixon Line — and sat on a bench with his hat on the ground in front of his feet and played, and played. By the end of the day there were usually enough pennies and nickels in his hat to buy his supper and the next day's food, but nothing more. This was not so bad though, for his relatives didn't come by much during the second half of the month because they knew that Vinny was broke and wouldn't be there anyway because he needed to work and earn a living.

Vinny carried on like this for a few years and his family grew and grew, and they spent more and more time with him during the first half of the month so that soon he was penniless after the first week of every month, which prompted him to hobble down to the Quarter now for three weeks or so every month and make music for money. During the fourth week of one month a few years after he returned to New Orleans, it occurred to Vinny that he probably had more relatives than anyone he knew and that somehow he needed to get away from them. Although he loved music, he hated making it for money. Music to him was part of his soul — it always had been, just as it had been for his granpappy who had taught him how to hold the harp and blow through it without spitting in it too much, and how to put the sounds together until you were making a song — your song — and using this as a way to tell people what was in your soul.

But doing this for money was kind of like prostituting — at least that's the way Vinny felt at the time. And that's what finally made Vinny decide to do something about his relatives, or more precisely about his financial situation. He had to leave this town.

Vinny's veteran's payment came on the second day of every month, or on the last day of the month if that was a Friday. The month after he made his decision was one of those Friday months, and this helped him a bit. His closest relatives would usually begin to show up during the afternoon of the second day of the month to check on Vinny's welfare and this would usually continue for about a week. He had never told his relatives that his money came early if the last day of the month was on Friday. The government had made arrangements for Vinny to pick up his money at a bank on the date that it was to be paid to him. This month he had laid his plans carefully. For the last two months he had even cut back drastically on his eating and had saved every penny he could from playing his harp.

On Friday morning when he got out of bed he put everything he had except his crutches into his army duffel bag and set it by his door. He took his crutches and made his way to the bank and collected his payment for the next month which began the next day, Saturday morning. He walked back toward his room and along the way he stopped a carriage and hired it to take him to the train station by way of his residence. The driver took him back to his room and fetched his bag for him. Vinny went to his landlady and paid the next week's rent just in case he needed to come back for some reason. He told her he was taking a little vacation up in the mountains. She told him that was fine by her and that she hoped he enjoyed himself and maybe he could bring her back a little something from the mountains because she had never been able to get away to the mountains. Vinny said sure.

He arrived at the train station and the driver took his bag to the baggage room. Vinny thanked him and paid him and then bought a one-way ticket to Asheville, North Carolina, and boarded his train.

When he arrived in Asheville early Monday morning he asked a Negro porter if there were any boarding houses near downtown that would welcome a man of color from New Orleans.

—You got any money? the porter asked.

—I do indeed, said Vinny. He showed the porter the wad of bills that he had just received from the government, and a little leather bag that was full of silver and copper coins.

—I'd say Miss Sophie would be glad to take you on, but you better let me walk you over there and take that bag for you. And you better not be showing that money around or you won't have it long in this town.

Miss Sophie's Room & Board was only a little over two blocks from the depot. The porter hoisted Vinny's bag onto a small wagon and invited Vinny to sit on it for the two block trip to the boarding house.

—No thanks. I'll take these here crutches and walk right along with you.

Thus it was that Vincent Bossard moved from the Quarter in New Orleans into Miss Sophie's Room

& Board in Asheville, North Carolina, where he lived the rest of his life.

Settling In At Miss Sophie's, Asheville 1920s

Vinny settled in to his room at Miss Sophie's, and the first morning there he wrote a letter to the tobacco company in Durham informing them that he had moved to Asheville and provided them with his new address. He then spent about a week getting used to Miss Sophie's cooking, which was not hard to do. She didn't cook cajun, but she knew how to cook. At every noon and evening meal she put out at least two meats and three or four vegetables. The boarders ate at one long table family style, and filled their plates family style. In fact, as the days passed, Vinny began to feel like he was part of a family at Miss Sophie's place. There was another colored person there, a young school teacher, and she was one of three females that stayed at the boarding house. There were five men.

Miss Sophie made some modifications to the house so that there were nine rooms to let which meant that each boarder had a private room. She installed a sink in each room to take some pressure off the three bathrooms that were available to the boarders. She had her own separate two-room apartment just off the kitchen and her own bathroom. The two full bathrooms upstairs were designated for the three ladies, and the five men shared the full bath downstairs and the water closet. She provided a chamber pot with a lid to each resident for use in each room. Rent included a weekly change of bed and bath linens and the laundry of these items. In cold weather Miss Sophie put what she called a feather bed in each room. This was what many in the north called a comforter, which might be described as a huge pillow — way bigger than the bed — that was stuffed with feathers which one could hardly stand to sleep under except in the most frigid weather. If the weather was not below zero — and it rarely was — most residents put a sheet on top of the feather bed and slept on it instead of under it. This is probably how it came to be known as a feather bed in the south.

If a renter wanted Miss Sophie to do his or her laundry she provided that service as well at a price that was competitive with the local laundries, and included ironing. Her residents were well fed and quite comfortable in their living conditions.

Miss Sophie made it clear when she interviewed an applicant that there were plenty of good boarding houses in the area, and that if one was uncomfortable eating at the same table or living in the same house as a person of another color, or even a Cherokee, then they should seek room and board elsewhere. Her boarding house was open to anyone she chose and that was that.

As far as Vinny could tell, that was fine with everyone there. Her rooms were always occupied, and there appeared to be a waiting list. The only complaint that he ever heard about the arrangements at Miss Sophie's was that it was almost impossible to keep from putting on weight if one stayed there for any length of time. In fact, the food was so good that she put in a second long table in the dining room and accepted day boarders for breakfast and dinner, essentially doubling her clientele except for supper. It may not have been a restaurant officially, but it was a fully integrated southern eating establishment as early as the 1920's.

Vinny began to get fat. Every morning he ate a breakfast that consisted of eggs and sausage and ham and fried pork chops and fried chicken, and often fried tenderloin chips and grits and some of the best biscuits that he had ever tasted. Miss Sophie had a Negro lady, Jamie, that helped her cook and she made the biscuits. She made these with lard and buttermilk and white flour, and occasionally delighted the guests with biscuits that had copious amounts of hog cracklins mixed in. These were the solids that remained in the bottom of the lard vat when chunks of fat were thrown into the cast iron pot and rendered over fire into lard. In Vinny's opinion few experiences in life were as sublime as biting into a hot biscuit that was filled with cracklins and slowly chewing it, and then washing it down with hot black coffee. After breakfast he either settled into the parlor and listened to the conversations of those who remained at the house — which were few because most had some kind of daytime occupation — or went to the front porch and rocked the morning away, watching the world go by.

By noon he could not truthfully say that he was hungry but the aromas coming out of the kitchen coupled with the arrival of the noon eaters urged him back to the dining room table. So he went, and he ate, and then he rocked the afternoon away on the porch and watched the world go by some more. And then he went back to the table at supper time and ate his evening meal. Vinny was happy, and getting fatter.

What more could a man want? His room and his board and his laundry consumed barely a third of his monthly payment from the government. His cigars cost him nothing because of the nice tobacco company in Durham. He had already received his first shipment of these at his new address because he had notified them of his change of address as soon as he got to Asheville. They had even thrown in some extra cigars with a note congratulating Vinny on his move to North Carolina.

At this point none of his funds were diverted to any of the Bossards in New Orleans, who he knew must be experiencing a dearth of funds for their daily needs, but he could not concern himself with that. They would just have to make do themselves, perhaps even go to work. Here he was happy, the residents liked him and were friendly to him, and most of them called him Uncle Vinny, which pleased him immensely. He had turned fifty a few weeks after he arrived at Miss Sophie's, and she had thrown a party for him after supper on his birthday. All the residents were there and each of them gave him a little something. And then he gave each of them a fresh cigar, including the women, and invited everyone to join him on the porch for a smoke. Two of the ladies politely declined, but to his utter amazement and joy, the young Negro teacher lady said sure she'd love to smoke a cigar with him on the porch, and she did. And then Miss Sophie came out to the porch with a tray that had a decanter and several small glasses on it and proposed that everyone serve themselves and raise a toast to Uncle Vinny, which they did, including the teacher lady, who sat in a rocking chair next to Vinny. When everyone exclaimed how good and how smooth the whiskey was, Miss Sophie explained that she had received it as an offering from one of her early suitors up in Murphy — or actually way up in the mountains outside of Murphy, and that it was at least fifteen years old and that she couldn't think of anyone she would rather share it with than Uncle Vinny and his friends on this very special evening. With a twinkle in her eye she said that she doubted that its makers had paid taxes on it, but what did that matter

— it was delicious, taxed or not. Uncle Vinny was happy, and because he was getting fat just sitting here on the porch, he determined that beginning the next day he would take his crutches and make his way to the courthouse lawn and sit on a bench for the morning, weather permitting. This would give him some exercise that he was not getting at the moment. He explained this to the teacher lady and she told Vinny she thought that was a great idea. When she told him she needed to turn in because she had to deal with twenty-five teenagers all day the next day she didn't call him Uncle Vinny — she just called him Vinny. He thanked her for smoking the cigar with him and she said she was the one that needed to thank him and that maybe they could do it again sometime. She went back in the house and Miss Sophie poured him another glass of that delicious Appalachian Mountain nectar, and Vinny was happy. He was home.

One morning about three months after moving from New Orleans to Asheville, Vinny left the breakfast table at Miss Sophie's Room and Board and went to his room and loaded a little sack that he usually carried slung over his shoulder. He made his way down the front steps and the path to the sidewalk and headed for the courthouse which was about four blocks away.

He had already made the trip three times, but did not tarry there on the earlier trips. Today would be different. He decided he needed to spend more time away from Miss Sophie's front porch. He moved along at a nice pace with his crutches and arrived at the courthouse lawn a few minutes later. There were several benches on the lawn. Vinny picked out one that faced south. It was under a big oak tree which would provide him shade in the summer time and a warming sun during cold weather. During his earlier surveillance trips he noted that this bench was never occupied, so he decided to claim it today by possession and use.

Vinny's first visitors were some pigeons and squirrels who came claiming some offering or another for use of the bench. He crumbled one of the biscuits in his bag and tossed the crumbs to the pigeons, and to the squirrels he tossed a handful of unshelled peanuts that he had taken from his personal stash. He liked to watch them go through the shelling process before eating them or stuffing them into their cheeks.

These visitors drifted away after Vinny finished feeding them, and Vinny sat and watched the world go by. At about nine o'clock a string of jailhouse inmates dressed in black and white striped jail attire hobbled from the jail on the other side of the square to a side door on the ground level of the courthouse. One deputy sheriff led them, and one followed with a shotgun. No one tried to escape and it appeared to Vinny that most of them seemed to enjoy being outside for the brief walk to the courthouse. Some of them even waived at Vinny and he smiled and waved back. You might say these were Vinny's second visitors, although they were not able to draw near to him at the time because of their chains. But that would change for some of them.No one else came that morning, and shortly before noon Vinny left his bench and crutched back to his room. He joined the regulars in the dining room and ate a big lunch and then made his way back to the courthouse for the afternoon. He was determined to set up a schedule and follow it as long as the weather permitted, for he knew he would need some time to get acclimated to the weather in the North Carolina highlands as opposed to the mild winters in New Orleans.

His bench was still available so he made his way over there and claimed it. The pigeons and squirrels immediately came over to demand the afternoon rent, which Vinny happily paid.

About half an hour later a deputy walked over from the jail. He was a big white man — tall and muscular — big.

—Howdy.

—Howdy Sir, said Vinny. He touched the brim of his hat.

—Ain't never seen you around here before have I?

—I doubt it — today's the first time I've been here to sit and stay awhile, although I've walked downtown a few times.

—Where ya comin' from?

—I moved up here from New Orleans about three months ago.

—And you ain't been in jail yet?

Vinny laughed. —Naw, and the good Lord willin' I don't plan to visit your facility any time soon.

—Don't be sayin' nothin' bad about our jail. We feed'em good in there. We even got some that won't stay out. They come in and do their ten days and when we turn'em loose and make'em leave they walk two blocks down the street and steal a pouch of tobacco right in front of the store owner and sit there til one of the city boys gets there. He brings'em back and books'em and they ain't missed a meal. How'd ya lose ya leg?

—Lost it in the war in Cuba in '99.

—You sleepin' on the streets?

—Naw, I'm staying at Miss Sophie's Room and Board.

—Ah, Miss Sophie's — the only intergrated place in town. I reckon you got a pension of some kind? We got a loiterin' law here.

—That's right. I been blessed with a small pension that gives me way more'n I need.

The deputy nodded.

—I've et over at Miss Sophie's a time or two. Don't matter to me if there's Negroes or Cherokee in there. The food takes care o' that. If ya let'er know a day ahead of time ya want to eat dinner there, she'll feed ya, for a quarter. A man cain't do better'n that.

—No Sir Sheriff, you got that right. Would you care to join me for a cigar? He reached into his bag and extended a cigar to the deputy.

—Naw, I gotta get back. The sheriff just wanted me to come over and check on ya and make sure nobody's messin' with ya.

—Well here, take this one and take one to the sheriff and tell'im I said I sure appreciate it. He handed the two cigars to the deputy.

—Thank ya. I'll tell'im. What's yore name?

—Vincent Bossard, but everybody calls me Vinny.

The deputy stared at him for a moment.

—Well I'm gonna call ya Uncle Vinny if that's alright by you. You look like you're about twicet my age, and that's the way my family raised me, don't matter what color ya are.

Vinny smiled.

—I would be honored. And what's your name if I may ask?

The deputy looked at the ground and kicked a dirt clod with the toe of his boot.

—Vincent Sewell.

Vinny smiled again.

—And what do people call you?

The deputy waited a moment and then kicked another dirt clod and looked off toward the jail before answering.

—Vinny, he said, and then they looked at each other and both broke out laughing, knee slapping, belly wrenching, lung wheezing hard.

Thus it was that Deputy Vinny and Uncle Vinny bonded with each other. The deputy was Uncle Vinny's third visitor, and the first who had a philosophical exchange with him on the courthouse lawn. From that moment forward, deputy Vinny would have taken a bullet for Uncle Vinny.

The Boarding House Receives an Unusual Guest

Sophie rose for the day at four-thirty and walked up the stairs of her boarding house to check the four rooms on the second floor. All four doors were closed and the bathroom was empty. She went back down the stairs and checked on the five rooms down there that she rented to her male guests. All appeared to be well. Miss Sophie's foremost concern was to make sure that her guests were comfortable in their rooms, that they were well fed in the dining room, and that they paid their rent in advance on the first day of the month without fail.

Sophie kept one room upstairs, the fourth room, that she would not rent long term because she wanted to be able to provide lodging to ladies passing through town, or passing through a difficult moment in their lives, who needed a room temporarily. The other three rooms upstairs she was willing to rent long term if that's what the guests wanted. They usually stayed occupied, and if a lady who had rented the temporary room needed to make her stay more or less permanent, Sophie would move her into the first permanent room that became available upstairs so that she could free up the temporary room for ladies who urgently needed a place to stay for a few nights for whatever reason.

There were several boarding houses in Asheville, but Sophie's was the only integrated one at the time. Sophie maintained good relations with the proprietors of these other establishments, and when a young lady appeared at her front door needing lodging, and Sophie's fourth room was unavailable, she could almost always make arrangements to place the young lady in a nearby room.

When the fourth room was available, Sophie was not nearly as strict about rent when a woman needed the room. She would discreetly inquire about the woman's financial situation, but her decision to accommodate the applicant was not based on her ability to pay. If the woman was penniless, Sophie always assured her that she could earn her keep for a few nights by assisting in the kitchen and with other tasks around the house.

Another concession that she made with regard to the fourth room was that she would allow two guests to occupy it at a time. And she made this clear to everyone who asked to rent the room for a few nights. She had two beds in the room, so the guests didn't have to share a bed. This enabled her to keep the rent lower for that room, and to accommodate more ladies who needed her assistance for temporary lodging. Sophie had been doing this for years, and she had never had a real problem with ladies taking advantage of her. She accomplished this by making it clear from the start that rental of the fourth room was temporary, and by maintaining a working relationship with various agencies and churches and others who would assist women who needed their assistance.

Over the years Sophie had lodged some unusual ladies in the fourth room. One time a few years back, a lady in her late twenties rang the doorbell at nine o'clock in the evening. Sophie came to the door and led her into the parlor. The young lady explained that she needed a place to stay for about a week and then she would be heading out to Abilene where her brother had assured her that she could find work. Sophie told her that the rent for the room would be six dollars for the week and that if she wanted board as well that would be another four dollars. The young lady retrieved a coin purse from her bag and took out 10 silver dollars.

She left before breakfast a week later, explaining to Sophie that she didn't have time for breakfast because she had to catch an early train. Sophie quickly packed her some ham biscuits to take along, for which the young lady thanked her. A half hour later when Sophie went to the fourth room to fetch the bed linens that the young lady had used, she found a pile of twenty dollar bills, fifty of them. A note was pinned to the top bill:

Thank you for your wonderful hospitality. It's been a very long time since I have experienced family as I have for the past week at your place. I leave this offering with the request that you use it to assist persons in need who may come your way. I trust your judgment in its use.

There was no signature. Since that day, every year on the first Monday in November, which was the day the young lady had caught her train to Abilene, a local lawyer has rung Sophie's front doorbell and handed her one thousand dollars in twenty dollar bills with a nice note in the handwriting of the young lady who had written the first note. After Vinny arrived, the note always inquired about him. This puzzled Sophie to no end, until she realized that this generous young lady must be sending a spy in to check on the place from time to time. Each year Sophie sent one hundred dollars to each of four other nearby boarding houses whose proprietors she knew assisted people who needed help. She never kept a penny of the yearly thousand dollars for herself, never paid any of it to herself as rent or board, but rather stuffed it into the pockets of her temporary guests as they left, based upon her perceptions of what they might need during the next stage of their journey, wherever that might be leading them. Many young ladies were surprised to find a twenty dollar bill with a note pinned to it in their pocket or purse after they were miles away from Miss Sophie's place. And this generosity was not limited to women. Sophie used the fifth room on the first floor for the same purposes as the fourth room upstairs, and when a young man, or an old one for that matter, who had stayed with Sophie for a few days while looking for work took his leave, he also often took a twenty dollar bill in one of his pockets or in the top of a paper bag in which Sophie had packed him some lunch, without knowing it until he was long gone from Miss Sophie's.

The high that Sophie experienced when she sent someone along with twenty dollars that he or she didn't know about was far better than anything she had experienced when pulling one of her long mountain drunks, or likkerin' up as they called it up in the real high country, before her granddaddy saved her by moving her to Asheville and setting her up with the boarding house.

It hadn't been easy getting to now. She had pulled a few drunks in Asheville too, but granddaddy had sent with her Jamie, the Negro cook who still lived with her and helped her run the boarding house; Jamie nursed her through the drunks, kept grandpa informed of her state, and kept the boarding house running while Sophie climbed back out of the black hole. After about six months of this Sophie decided to quit getting drunk, and she never got drunk again. That was behind her, and now she was experiencing a high that made the highs of the past pale in comparison.

Vinny's Next Door Neighbor

Vinny's next door neighbor at Miss Sophie's was a man who called himself a half breed because his mama was a full-blooded Cherokee and his daddy was full-blooded Scotch-Irish. He was a funny-looking fellow who looked distinctly Cherokee except that he had a tightly curled head of hair. He had a Bachelor of Arts degree from the University of North Carolina at Chapel Hill. One night during the fall that Vinny arrived in town, this neighbor, George Barnes, who had occupied the room right next to Vinny's for three years, completely upset the equilibrium at Miss Sophie's by coming home toting a basket with a baby in it.

George had been working as a librarian for several years at various venues, including the new junior college that had just been started up in Asheville. He made a decent living as a librarian, and his room at Miss Sophie's was his home. Over the last year or so he had spent most of his weekends away from the boarding house. He had missed the supper call this evening so he took the baby straight to the kitchen. The men who were sitting on the porch smoking and talking immediately got up and followed him into the kitchen to see what the baby was about. The ladies who had been sitting in the parlor talking, and two of whom were also smoking, got up and followed the men and George and the baby into the kitchen to see what the baby was about. There had never been this many people in the kitchen at one time, at least since Vinny got there because Sophie didn't permit the crowd to come into the kitchen. She would occasionally invite someone to step into the kitchen to sample some dish or to inquire about their day or some other event, but otherwise the kitchen was off limits to the crowd. Tonight when the baby came in she was not in the kitchen, but from her rooms next door she heard the commotion and went to see what was happening. She and Jamie got to the kitchen door at the same time.

George had set the basket with the baby in it on the work table and was inquiring about where he might find some milk for the baby. Jamie moved everybody aside and lifted the baby out of the basket. The baby looked like a little Cherokee baby —

especially with its thick black hair. Jamie looked at George and then back at the baby, and then whispered into Sophie's ear. Sophie looked at the baby's thick black hair, which was tightly curled like George's, and nodded.

—Where'd you get this baby, George?

—She's my baby, Miss Sophie.

Everybody hushed and listened.

—It's a girl?

—Yes ma'am.

—Why didn't you tell me you had a baby?

—It was kind of private and her mama still had her.

—What do you mean her mama still had her?

—She still had her till she got killed yesterday.

—Her mama got killed yesterday?

—Yes ma'am.

—Where?

—Up in Murphy. She was staying with some friends. That's where I've been goin' on Saturdays these last few months. We got married about a year and a half ago and we ended up with this baby. We even got married the county way. Her family said we didn't have to since we were Cherokee but we went through a Cherokee and a county ceremony anyway and we've got a certificate filed over in the Cherokee Records and at the courthouse. I've got a copy of the marriage certificate right here in my room. We were going to rent us a place here in Asheville as soon as I got enough money put away to start out on our own.

—How'd she get killed?

—A gang of boys jumped her and when they had all finished with her, they stabbed her. I got a telegram at the library today telling me to come get the baby before the law takes her. They haven't found the boys and nobody's sure they could identify them.

Everybody looked at George and then back at the baby, who appeared to be perfectly content in Jamie's arms.

—So this baby's how old?

—About five months. He swallowed hard. I'll find someplace else to stay; I can start looking tomorrow, but I need to feed her something now. If it's all right I'll just keep her in my room tonight. If I take her to any of the churches they'll call in the law, and I'm not going to let the law take my baby from me.

Everybody looked at Sophie and Jamie and the baby. Nobody said anything as they waited for Sophie's decision.

—What are ya'll starin' at? Get back out there where you're supposed to be — we gotta figure out what we're gonna do with this baby. George, you're not goin' anywhere for now — this baby needs her daddy right here with her. You got any diapers in that basket?

—They told me there were two extra ones in there, but they said they didn't have any milk to send. Her mama's been nursing her.

—Who's they?

—The Cherokee family that were lettin' her mama stay with them till we could get us a place here in Asheville.

—Well she very clearly needs a clean diaper now. I'll send Jamie for some in the morning and we'll make do tonight with what we have. I've got some soft dish towels that'll work just fine 'til we can get some diapers tomorrow. I've got some nipples in there that we can put on a juice bottle, and we've got plenty of canned milk. She's not gonna starve before mornin', and we'll decide then how we're gonna handle this. The law may come lookin' for her whether we like it or not. You make sure you can put your hands on that marriage certificate fast in case any of the state people come nosing around.

She reached for the baby and Jamie handed it to her.

—Yep, she definitely needs her diaper changed. George, she can stay here in your room with you, but I think you ought to let her stay in Jamie's room tonight. Jamie knows how to take care of these little ones, and you're gonna need some sleep. And as far as tomorrow goes, you go on back to work. This baby'll be safe right here 'til you can come back home to her.

—Yes ma'am. Thank you Miss Sophie.

She pressed the baby's head into the crook of her neck and turned away from the crowd for a moment. Then she handed the baby back to Jamie and brushed the tears from her cheeks.

Jamie took the baby and held it against her neck just like Sophie had done.

—George, if you need to see this baby anytime during the night you just come knock on my door, you hear me?

—Yes, Jamie. Thank y'all so much. You may not know it, but my baby is the most important thing in the world to me. I loved her mama, and it hurts so much.

And that's when he broke down crying, and that's when Jamie and Sophie broke down crying, and after a few moments Sophie told him he should go on out to the parlor to settle down for awhile before bedtime, or if he wanted to maybe he ought to go ahead and settle down in his room.

—We need to take care of this baby now and us standin' around crying is not helping much. Jamie'll bring the baby in there so you can tell her good night before she puts her to bed.

—Thank you Miss Sophie. I believe I'll just go on to my room now. You got a chicken leg or a pork chop I could take in there with me? I'm kind of hungry now that I've got the baby here.

—Oh my! I forgot about you needin' to eat too! I'll fix you a whole plate. You want to eat in the dining room?

—No ma'am, I don't believe I could handle the company right now. But I would appreciate it if you'd tell everybody out there what you decided. You know we're all kind of one big family here and they'll want to know.

—I'll go out there and tell'em. They're probably listenin' through the walls anyway, but I'll tell'em so we can all get some sleep tonight.

She started toward the parlor and then stopped and turned to George. —What's her name?

George hesitated and looked at the floor before answering. —We named her Sophia Adsila Barnes the night she was born at the hospital. We wanted her to be the kind of person you are Miss Sophie. I had told my wife all about you. That's the name we told the doctor to put on the birth certificate. Adsila means blossom.

Sophie turned away from him. After a few moments she turned back to George and looked him in the eye. Then she went back into Jamie's room and told her to go out there and tell everybody what they had decided to do with the baby for now. She just couldn't face that crowd in the dining room.

The Day After The Baby Arrived

The next morning everybody got up a little earlier than usual. They all looked down the hall toward Jamie's room and stuck their heads in the kitchen to see if the baby was up and about, and then took to their normal morning routines. Cold weather had not set in yet, so some of the men turned on the porch lights and sat out there for their first smokes of the day. This caused the neighbors on each side of Miss Sophie's house to stick their heads out their front doors to see what was going on, what with everybody being on the porch a half hour early. Upstairs, the ladies stirred early too, and one could hear the clinking of the little bottles in their toiletries and soon the air was mixed with the smell of their perfumes and the aroma of the cigarette smoke from the smokers who had remained in the parlor, and the morning was alive.

Each morning Miss Sophie or Jamie rang a little bell when they were ready for the residents to come to the breakfast table. They rang the bell a little early this morning and everybody hurried into the dining room. As they ate, everybody kept looking toward the kitchen door to see if Jamie or Sophie would bring the baby in so it could join everyone for breakfast. After everyone had settled in and begun to eat, Jamie walked into the room with a bundle in her arms, and as she set it in George's arms a big black mop of curly hair began to stir and she let out a loud yell.

—What's wrong with the baby? they all asked.

—Ain't nothin' wrong with that baby, said Jamie, She's just tellin' y'all good mornin'!

Everybody said good morning back to the baby, and George looked proud and happy, this even though he had lost the baby's mama two days before. He wondered about the feelings he was having. He had loved the woman. They could sit quietly for hours and not talk and yet feel peace in each other's presence. And they had made this child together, and had told each other that it was their child and that they would always take care of each other and the child, and the monsters had killed her and now only he had the baby, and when he thought about her mama he felt empty and angry. The young mama would not see her baby flower into the person that George had determined that he would help her become. And so he held the baby, and at the same time that he felt this deep, empty sadness and anger, he also felt an inexplicable joy and happiness as he rubbed his hand over the little girl's mop of thick, black, curly hair.

Everybody had forgotten about their food. Sophie stood at the head of the table next to the kitchen door as Jamie touched George on the shoulder and reached down and took the bundle from him. The bundle yelled again, and Jamie and Sophie smiled and said she was just telling everybody she was just as hungry as they were, so everybody needed to get on with their breakfast and they would feed the baby in the kitchen. So everybody got back to their breakfast and coffee and began to comment about what a fine baby that was and what a head of hair she had and where was she going to stay, in George's room or in Jamie's room? Or maybe she should have her own room. They could switch rooms around some so that the baby could have the little room next to Jamie's and George could have the room next to that so that the baby would be in a room between George and Jamie. There was already a door between Jamie's room and the baby's, and they could easily put in a door between the baby's room and George's new room. One of the ladies suggested that maybe the baby should stay upstairs since she was a girl and that's where the females stayed, but that didn't go very far. The consensus was that the baby was still George's baby and that she should stay by him. And thus the crowd at Miss Sophie's Room & Board spent the rest of breakfast time determining what changes would need to be made there at the house for their new baby.

Every time they heard a yell from the kitchen, they moved ahead with greater resolve.

Vinny's New Leg

About the time the baby arrived, another major change was taking place in town: the government was giving Vinny a new leg. He had gone for years without an artificial leg, partly because he didn't want one and partly because the army people down in New Orleans didn't push for it. After all, they were costly.

But the situation in Asheville was different. The government fellow who took care of Vinny's records here and who made sure he received his pension payment every month had convinced Vinny that he ought to give the leg a try. And so he had agreed, and today, the day after the baby arrived, Vinny went to the medical office that would fit the new leg on him and coach him and teach him how to use it until he felt comfortable and balanced with the new appliance. He spent the morning there getting the leg fitted and then walking around the walls of the room holding a handrail on the wall. Although his stump was perfectly healed — it had had years to heal — it was very tender and sore by the time he finished his first exercises with the staff at the medical office. He had expected to take his leg home with him, but they told him it would be a few days before he could do that because he needed the practice and he needed to toughen up the fleshy part of his stump that came into contact with the leg so that he would no longer feel any soreness.

After three hours at the clinic, Vinny crutched back to his room in time for dinner, where the baby was still the center of attention. The non-resident regulars who took their noon meal at Miss Sophie's now found themselves to be additionally differentiated from the residents by this unusual fact: no matter how intrigued they were by the new baby, since they didn't live at the boarding house, they couldn't claim this baby as their baby. The language of the residents was full of the first person plural — We're gonna cut a door between his room and her room; we'll keep her in diapers, you don't need to worry about that; we're not gonna let anything happen to our baby — the law ain't got no right to come take'er from us.

And so by this attitude the baby was incorporated into the family immediately. Everyone respected the fatherhood of George, and the rights attendant to that status, and not a one of them would have attempted to block George from taking the baby from the house and going elsewhere. But that issue had been settled by the matriarch of the family and her helper. The baby was staying here, and so it was their baby, to be cared for by them, to be financed by them, to be guarded by them from the impositions of the outside world.

Vinny knew nothing of Sophie's charitable account, or of her blessings to certain sojourners at the house — even the sojourners didn't know about it until they were long gone. And so he had no idea that the baby's financial needs were already met. But something in him stirred and made him commit then and there to use whatever funds he needed from his growing savings account to make sure this baby lacked nothing. And so it was with everybody else at the boarding house. Not a one of them was rich, but they were all — men and women — wage earners who had a little margin in their finances. Without consulting each other at all, they all allocated in their spirit a portion of their cushion to their new baby. They did this without even thinking about it. It was just there, this commitment — unreferenced, unspoken, undefined: this baby was not going to go hungry, no sir. And although she no longer had a breast to suck on, she'd have plenty of bodies there at the boarding house to keep her warm and happy. And she was going to have clothes as good as those of any other baby in town, and if she got sick there was going to be money to pay the doctor's bill, yessiree.

Something welled up in the women at the house, making them want to hold the baby and cuddle her against their breasts and feed her and keep her clean and warm; and something made the hair rise on the necks of the men because they felt mad and protective when they imagined various harms that some outsider might wish to visit upon their baby. Somebody could get killed if they tried to come in here and hurt this baby. Such was the commitment of the residents of the boarding house to Sophia. It was immediate and it was not reasoned. It sprang from within their usness, and it was just there, and it was not in the outsiders, in those who did not reside in their house.

Vinny's stump was sore. He had spent almost three hours that morning wearing his new leg and putting weight on it as he moved around the training room. But he was determined to go back this afternoon and practice some more; his goal was to begin wearing his leg all day within a few days, and to lay aside his crutches within a month. The doctor had told him that he was going to have to completely relearn how to balance himself when he walked, because he didn't have toes on his stump side and that's one of the main functions of toes, besides stinking. This tickled Vinny when the doctor said it, and he determined that he was going to relearn balancing with his artificial leg as quickly as he could. So that afternoon he went back to the clinic and spent another two hours walking on his new leg. He was making progress. They told him he could take his leg home with him the next week if he wasn't too sore, but that he should count on using his crutches for another month or two along with his leg until he was totally comfortable with his balance. Today Vinny left his leg at the clinic after another two hours of work there, and crutched directly to his bench on the courthouse lawn, where he paid his rent to the squirrels and pigeons and lit up a well-earned cigar.

So Vinny's life changed that fall in two significant ways: he obtained and learned to use an artificial leg, which he came to like, and he became an undeclared protector of a new person in the household, a baby named Sophia.

Nobody Could Sleep

Nobody could sleep. It was already ten o'clock and the neighborhood was dark and the evening sounds had waned and the night had settled outside, but not here inside Miss Sophie's place. Sophia the baby wouldn't stop yelling. This was disconcerting not only to George but to the whole household. George had essentially relinquished the charge of his baby to Jamie, who was now in the room next to his trying to comfort the baby, but nothing was working. And by now every person in the house had developed a kind of parental relationship with the baby, and so its cries tonight kept them awake not by the noise but because of their protective instincts and urges toward the infant.

Not a person in the house would have tried to prevent George from taking his baby and moving somewhere else if that was what he determined to do. But that was not on the table. This was George's family. The baby had been in the house now for several weeks, and everybody who lived there had developed a relationship with her that caused them to have urges to succor — to surround and protect and nourish this baby that was now their baby, at least for a time.

George tapped on the door.

—Come on in George.

Jamie was holding Sophia and rocking her in her arms.

—You reckon she's hungry? he asked.

—No, we've fed her and she took a whole bottle. And she had a good burp. She may have a little colic, but I don't think so. Sometimes babies just need to cry.

A Government Lady Comes To The House

About two months after the baby arrived, Sophie's grandpa and grandma came for a visit. Sophie had written them about the baby, and her letter had been full of excitement. They decided to come down and visit Sophie and see her new boarder.

Just as they drove up and parked in front of the boarding house, about mid-morning, Deputy Vinny pulled up in his patrol car and parked right behind them. He greeted them and followed them up the steps to the front porch. They went in, and he lingered and after a moment he rang the front door bell. Sophie came to the door and greeted him.

—How's it goin' Vinny? Don't tell me you're wantin' to eat dinner here today?

He laughed. —Naw, I just need to speak to Uncle Vinny for a minute if he's around. But how about tomorrow?

—I'll set a place for you. Let me go see if Vinny's in his room. Come on in.

A few moments later Vinny came out and the deputy suggested they go out and talk on the porch.

—Uncle Vinny, I need to tell you something. We got a call this morning from the Social Services people up in Murphy asking about the baby.

—What'd they want?

—I'm not sure, but it sounds like they think the county should take custody of her.

—Why would they think that?

—I don't know. I heard the sheriff tell'em the baby's staying with her daddy and that they've got a good comfortable place to stay. He told'em George has a full-time job and they said that's the problem — she don't have nobody to stay with during the day while he's at work.

—That's crazy! She's got Miss Sophie and Jamie here all day every day during the week, and her daddy of an evening and on the weekends. Them two ladies are not going anywhere what with having to cook three meals a day every day.

—I know. I just wanted to let you know there may be some trouble. You might want to warn George and Miss Sophie before them Social Services people come down here and start pokin' around.

—I will. Is that all you know about it?

—Yep, that's it for now. I'll letcha know if I hear anything else.

He couldn't imagine this happening in New Orleans, especially among his people. If a parent died, the other parent took care of the child, and family and friends stepped in as needed. Unless there was clear evidence that the baby was being mistreated or neglected, the people felt that who raised the child was none of the state's business. This baby clearly was not being mistreated or neglected. She was happy, fat, comfortable, and loved by a houseful of people that had suddenly become her family.

He found Jamie in the kitchen.

—Where's Miss Sophie?

—She's back in her apartment with her grandma and grandpa. You need to talk to her?

—I think so. The deputy just told me that the state people from Murphy called and asked about the baby and wanted to know where they could find it.

Sounds like they're talking about putting the baby in foster care until George can prove that he's fit to take care of her and is making sure she's being taken care of while he's at work.

—George don't have to prove nothin'! snapped Jamie. He's that baby's daddy and he's taking good care of her. But she knew that Vinny was right to be worried. George was a nobody to the state. Over the last years the state had built up its bureaucracies to the extent that they had to go out among the people looking for problems, so they could find work enough to justify their continued existence. For the most part these bureaucracies and their bureaucrats were worthless, fulfilling no valid social function whatsoever. Their concern was not the welfare of this baby but rather the power they could exert in the circumstances. She could feel this in her bones.

—I'll tell Sophie to step out here for a minute. You want to talk to her folks too?

—It don't matter. I'm sure she'll tell'em if I don't.

Jamie stepped out of the kitchen and in a few moments came back with Sophie and her grandparents. —Vinny, tell'em what you just told me.

Vinny told them. The old man and his woman nodded. Sophie stepped into the baby's room and came back with Sophia in her arms. Grandma reached for the baby and took it.

—If they've gone this far they'll try to take this baby, said Jeremiah. Not that they care about the baby or her daddy — they don't. But they'll follow their policies. That keeps'em funded.

—Miss Sophie, I think we better call George at the library and tell him what's going on, said Vinny. For all we know they may be on the way from Murphy right now. We know for sure they've already called the sheriff asking where they can find the baby.

—I'll call him, said Sophie, but I think maybe the baby better take a ride for a little while, like maybe for a routine checkup at the doctor's office. I'll take her and let Jamie take care of dinner and supper today. It may take me awhile to find a doctor that can see her, so I wouldn't be surprised if I'm gone pretty much the whole rest of the day.

~ ~ ~

Not ten minutes after Sophie drove away with the baby a black sedan parked at the curb in front of the boarding house, and a woman dressed in dark blue business attire got out of the car and came to the front door and rang the bell. Jamie came to the door.

—May I help you?

—I need to speak with Mr. George Barnes.

—I'm sorry, he's not here right now.

—But he lives here?

—Yes, he does.

—And does he have a baby?

—Yes he does.

—And the baby lives here with him?

—Yes, the baby lives here. May I ask the purpose of your visit?

—I'm with the Department of Social Services over in Cherokee County and I have an administrative order authorizing me to take the child into protective custody. Please take me to the baby. She stepped closer to the door.

Jamie didn't move. —The baby is not here.

—Where is she?

—I don't know, said Jamie. The owner of this boarding house took her for a routine medical checkup, but she said she was going to have to look around for a doctor, so I can't tell you where she is.

—I don't believe you. Step aside, I want to look inside.

Jamie still didn't move. —I don't think that would be appropriate. I've told you the baby is not here.

—It doesn't matter what you think. I have a legal authorization to take that baby into custody and I am going to take her to Murphy with me this afternoon. Step aside.

Jamie blocked her way.

—If you don't move, I am going straight to the sheriff and have him come back over here with me and enforce this authorization.

Jamie still didn't move.

—Very well, I shall be back shortly. She turned and walked briskly to her car.

Jamie went to the phone and called the sheriff's office and asked for deputy Vinny.

—You were right. She's here to pick up the baby. I wouldn't let her in, and I told her the baby is not here right now. In fact I told her the truth but she didn't believe me, so now she's on her way to your office to get someone to come back over here with her and take the baby.

—Did Miss Sophie take her to the doctor? I heard her say something about that awhile ago.

—Yes, but I have no idea which doctor.

—I'll put out an all points bulletin on the radio and see if we can find her or her car. It shouldn't be too hard. Everybody here knows Miss Sophie, and every deputy knows her car. Half of'em are lustin' after her. We'll take our time sending somebody back with this woman. As understaffed as we are today it could easily take an hour and a half before we can send anybody over there with her. We'll let Miss Sophie know what's going on as soon as we find her. One of us will be over there in a little while with this woman, so we'll try to make sure Miss Sophie doesn't come home any time soon.

Sophie drove around town trying to figure out what she should do. It certainly would be a good time to take the baby for a medical checkup but it might be more important to get the baby to her daddy and let him decide what to do. She could drive out to the college library and talk to him there. She could get a student to go in and tell him to come to the car.

She drove to the next corner and just as she turned, a city police car pulled behind her and turned on his flashing light. She pulled to the curb and the officer pulled in behind her. She recognized him when he walked up to her car.

—Miss Sophie do you have the baby with you?

—I do.

—There's a woman here in town from social services who says she has an authorization to take the baby into custody.

—Did you pull me over to help her do that?

—You know better than that Miss Sophie. I just wanted to tell you that one of your tires looks a little low.

—Thanks, Tim.

—And if you don't mind tell Jamie to set me a place for dinner tomorrow if you have room.

—I'll do it. Thanks again.

She pulled back into the street and headed toward the college. She knew she had to talk to George. They were going to have to figure some way to keep this baby away from the boarding house and get her out of town, today, unless George just wanted to let the state take custody of her. She doubted that was the case.

George trotted out to the car and got in. Sophie drove as she told him what had happened.

—It's your call George. You're her daddy.

George was nervous. —I better go tell the boss I need to take the rest of the day off. He'll let me do that I'm sure.

She took him back to the library and George spoke to his boss and then they drove into the countryside on the east side of town.

—We'll do whatever you want George. We can even get you out of the state if we need to. We can be in Tennessee or South Carolina or even Georgia by this afternoon.

Sophie had the baby on the seat between them. George looked at her. His guts were churning.

—They're not gonna take this baby if I can help it. She's never been mistreated, she's never gone hungry. Look at her — look how fat she is! And she sure doesn't lack for company. Everybody at the house holds her and feeds her, and all the girls there change her diapers. I even saw Vinny change her diaper the other day.

—George, sometimes people that work for the government get too much power and they start liking it and it drives'em. Then they start believing they're right. And that's when we start having trouble.

Sophie pulled up to the gas pump at a country gas station and the owner came out and pumped gas, checked her oil, and cleaned her windshield. She paid and pulled back onto the road and kept driving.

—It's your call George. The tank's full and the road's wide open. I'm sure that woman is still waiting at the sheriff's office. Or we can go back to the house if you want to fight it here in Asheville or Murphy.

He sat quietly for a minute or two as they continued along a country road. He clearly didn't know what to do, but he had decided that he was going to keep his baby. The decision was made. He must focus now on how best to do that. The solution came as a complete shock to him.

Sophie pulled over onto a wide shoulder and stopped. She turned toward George.

—George, it's early in the day. We can be in Spartanburg in three hours. I've got a solution that will be good for this baby, and it will be good for you and me.

—What's that?

—We'll get married.

Silence…

—Married? He was stunned. He looked at her with his mouth hanging open.

—Yeah. My grandma and grandpa met on Monday and got married that Thursday. You and I have known each other a whole lot longer than that. And this baby will be our baby, and she'll have a daddy and a mama, and that should take the steam out of the social services people trying to take her. We'd make about as normal a couple as anybody could ask for. You're thirty-two and I'm twenty-nine. You've got a good job and I've got a good business. The house is paid for. I think they'd lose interest in trying to get her real quick if we're married. And even if they do keep coming after the baby, I don't believe there is a judge in the state that would allow it if we're married. And all I've heard so far is that there's an authorization. Nobody's said anything yet about an order from a judge commanding anyone to take the baby.

—Married? What about love?

—I already love this baby!

—No, I mean me.

—You know what, George? You're a good man, you're honest and hard-working, and even though you're highly educated you're not hifalutin. I've known you for years now. I really like you. I'm not sure there's a whole lot of difference between liking and loving. Right now liking is good enough for me. Do you like me?

—Of course I like you. What am I supposed to say — No I don't like you? Look how you've taken care of my baby over the last few weeks. But I'm having a hard time processing this. Half the bachelors in town would like to be sittin' here right now listenin' to you propose to'em, and how do I feel? I feel like I'm about to pass out! I'm losing my breath!

—Don't do that. We can turn around and go straight back home if that's what you want.

—I didn't say that. I just don't know what to say. Are you talking about this afternoon?

—Yes. We can be there in three hours, and in South Carolina we can get a marriage license and get married the same day. I think we can be in and out of the courthouse in less than an hour.

—I can't believe this.

—Do you want me to turn around?

—I didn't say that. I'm just having a hard time getting my head around this.

—I understand. The fact is, though, the authorities in Murphy are trying to take this baby, and this would throw up a barrier that I think would stop them. And I think it may have some nice side effects. That would include you and me spending the rest of our lives together.

He almost smiled. —You really like me? He was incredulous.

—I really like you.

He stared into the nearby woods. Maybe there was something to this notion that liking is more important than loving. He had seen couples who loved each other but who clearly didn't like each other. He had never thought about that before now, but it was clear that there was little happiness in those marriages. And he really did like Sophie. She had been good to him, had respected him, from the moment he had moved into her boarding house. She had a good heart. She was not afflicted with the racism that permeated society, and he had never heard her say anything that would indicate that she thought herself to be superior to others. That was something he admired.

He turned back to her. —You know I'm half Cherokee, right?

—You know I'm half wildcat, right?

He chuckled. —I'm beginning to see that. You know, don'tcha, that half the single guys in Asheville would give their eye teeth to be where I am right now?

—I have absolutely no interest in any of them. The only man I'm interested in is you.

—And that's because of my baby?

—That's a big part of it, yes. But I'll say it again, I really like you, and that's special for me.

—Should I still ma'am you and call you Miss Sophie?

She laughed. —No.

He looked down the road. —And you figure it's about three hours from here?

—I know it is.

—And what happens when we walk out of the courthouse?

—You'll be my husband. I'll be your wife. Use your imagination.

His head was spinning and his chest was pounding. He couldn't believe his ears.

—Let's go.

Near Asheville, Circa 2010 a.d.

The archbishop backslides in a season of folly, but is eventually rescued

Archie had two struggles that interfered with his ministry for a short time. One of these was a temptation to own a private jet to shuttle him around his huge diocese, like a handful of the televangelists who were raking in the gold. The other was that he couldn't get the armory out of his mind. He had always believed that a man, or a woman for that matter, should never be without a good steel blade and a top quality gun or two with sufficient ammunition to last a few years. And of late, as he matured in his responsibilities, he began to think more and more about the armory. The armory would be an institution that would insure that the community itself was properly armed and that there would be sufficient weaponry and ammunition to handle any situation that might arise. Every town in the archdiocese would have an armory. Of course the backwoods communities wouldn't need an armory. Practically every rural household in the mountains was an armory already. Archie loved these mountain households and looked forward to holding them up to the more urban populations as an example of how people ought to be prepared to protect themselves and hunt for their food if necessary, without giving much thought to the fact that there is not much wildlife in the towns and cities to be hunted. And so Archie spent many happy hours planning the development and placement of these armories as instruments of the church.

Archie loved to think about these things because his thoughts led him to a deep and compelling justification for both the development of the armory and for his desire to fly. His thinking would usually begin something like this: There are patterns and models in nature from which we can learn. For example, look at Proverbs chapter 30, and various other proverbs in that ancient book of wisdom that invoke these patterns by reference to various creatures in nature. One of his favorite creatures, though not mentioned in the Proverbs, was the wasp, because almost all big wasps have stingers, which is their equivalent of a blade or other weapon, he would say. Since some of the evolutionists claim that we are descended from low life forms, like wasps he would think, then we should probably emulate our wasp ancestors and have our stingers as well. His wife at first seemed to accede to this reasoning, although she told Archie she was a bit uncomfortable thinking that she may have descended from a wasp. But in fact she had, Archie pointed out in a moment of levity. Her great, great grandmother had moved to the Appalachian highlands from the Scottish highlands when she was just a child; she was clearly of ancient Scottish stock, and she had always attended a Presbyterian church of one sort or another until she died. Thus she was a WASP Archie gleefully told her, a White Anglo-Saxon Protestant!

Archie pointed out to his wife that the reasoning about the wasps even supported his thoughts about a private jet or helicopter: How? Wasps could fly!

When he shared this thinking with his wife, who had spent four years in the navy, she responded that he could already fly, that there were probably thousands of commercial flights every single day in his archdiocese, if he could call it that; to which he responded that every wasp had his own wings! To which she responded, switching to an Appalachian dialect that she had refined in the navy and which was understood by almost all Appalachians, that he should concern himself with the struggles of his bishops and his flock and that there was a scientific consensus that we descended from simians not wasps and that his very existence supported this theory and that the archbishop of Appalachia had of late become a complete idiot.

Archie had never served in the navy but he was an Appalachian so he understood the language that his wife used to communicate her views and admonitions. Rather than continuing the discussion he slinked out to the workshop at the back of his lot and spent the afternoon thinking about Proverbs 30 and 31 and working on his model airplane collection which included a Gulfstream 5 and several nice helicopters. When he returned to the house for supper that evening he discovered that his wife's car was gone and that she had arranged for him to have a time of fasting and solitude.

As the years passed and some of the televangelists went to prison, Archie slowly matured and his temptations waned, and he delighted more and more in the bride of his youth. She nurtured him, protected and guided him, kept him company, supported his illusions, and blocked him every time she thought it necessary to do so. She stayed a step ahead of him in every circumstance, like a guardian dog going ahead of the shepherd, alert, gathered, ready to kill. And then she died.

Archie was alone, but he was not lonely. He missed his wife, but he had matured in his commitment to serve the region known as Appalachia. In his earlier years this view could have almost been described as delusional and puerile, a religious fantasy, but as the troubles of the broader western society grew, Archie's commitment to his mission began to make more sense, not regarding institutional religious organization but in relation to raw, daily discipleship. In his maturity Archie embraced the apostle Paul's invocation of ancient scripture in his second letter to the Christians in Corinth that said:

I will live among them

and walk with them,

and I will be their God,

and they will be my people.

So,

Remove yourselves from them

and be separate,

says the Lord.

Do not embrace the unclean,

and I will take you in.

And,

I will be your Father,

and you will be my sons and daughters,

says the Lord Almighty.

Archie had spent years thinking about this passage. It was a call to God's people to be different, to separate themselves from the indulgent societies of which they were and are a part. He never saw Appalachia as a perfect place but he did see it as a rare place where the general society did not see or pursue salvation and life in the material. Appalachian society generally, with all its imperfections, accepted and nurtured the simple life, and understood and supported a person's rejection of material pursuits. Archie knew of no other place where this could be said of such a vast segment of the greater society. Over the years he had become comfortable with the idea that Appalachian culture could be defined as one that broadly accepts and fosters the fundamental teaching of Jesus that a person's life does not consist in an abundance of possessions. Life is not found in the material, in stuff. But the outside world was teaching otherwise, and as Archie saw it the modern institutional church had aligned itself with this worldly teaching, even in Appalachia. There was much work to be done. He would renew his mission as archbishop and get to work.

He would meet the poets and the ditch diggers and the mechanics and the fiddlers and the doctors and the preachers and the hippies and the writers and the grandmas and grandpas and the prisoners and the sheriffs and the farmers. He would eat with them and learn from them and cry with them and baptize them and bury them. He would teach others to do the same and he would do all within his power to set the right example. With the help of God, he would never again allow himself to be seduced by the allure of material possessions or the glitter of gold. He would spend his life living.

Uncle Billy,
Appalachia 2021

Not too far from Shanky Bottom, up the mountain a ways toward where the Zen man lives, there's an old black man that everybody calls Uncle Billy that lives in a little cabin on a white man's old family farm. Or at least it looks like Uncle Billy lives on the white man's farm. In fact, the white man, Zeb Polk, years ago deeded five acres to Uncle Billy free and clear. But just looking at it you would never know it because Uncle Billy's land sits right in the middle of the farm, not more than three or four minutes walking time from the main farm house that was built before the Civil War. The cabin was already over a hundred years old when Uncle Billy arrived from New Orleans back in the late 1970's bearing the name Guillaume Gaston LeClerq. The locals soon changed his name to Billy. As Billy became older, an older black man in the South, the appellation gradually changed to Uncle Billy, a name used by those with a soul to show respect and honor and dignity to an elderly human being. Uncle Billy loved this. It took him to his origins.

There is of course a back story here. Guillaume Gaston LeClerq is a man of letters. Uncle Billy has published two books of poetry, five novels, a treatise on the relations of universals and particulars from the perspective of a phenomenologist, and many scholarly articles. He publishes in French. In the academic season, he rises at 3:30 a.m. and has coffee and a light snack. At 4:30 a.m. he sits at a console and greets his students at the University of Paris via electronic conference. It is 10:30 a.m. in Paris. The seminar ends at noon Paris time. At 6:00 a.m. Appalachian time Billy's teaching day has ended and he walks from his cabin to the antebellum farm house and joins Zeb for breakfast.

Born in Paris in 1955 to intellectual French Africans who were career diplomats, Uncle Billy attended local French schools from age six, except for a four year stay in Toronto where his parents were assigned to a consortium of French African countries sharing space at the French consulate there. He attended English speaking schools in Toronto. He entered the Sorbonne in 1973. He left Paris for New Orleans in 1977, and spent two years refining his nearly perfect English and then moved to Zeb's place in 1979. Now in their mid-sixties, they are both old men, both old poets. Zeb's wife is in her last year of teaching high school and Guillaume's wife is dead, having passed away ten years back. She too was a poet, widely read in France and French Africa. To most of the mountain folks here, most, it appeared that Zeb had made friends with some black people when he had gone off to school and they had joined him on the old family farm not too long after he came back and he let them stay there and help take care of the place. Appalachians understand friendship.

Guillaume and Zeb met at the University of Paris in the 1970's where they were both studying European civilization and literature. Guillaume had engaged Zeb intellectually and they spent their student years talking and reading and writing poetry and exploring the whole world of ideas, including the cataclysmic changes that had recently occurred in European higher education, and in particular in France. After three years of friendship Zeb offered Guillaume a place on his farm in Appalachia, and told him he would build him a little house there. When Guillaume saw the little cabin on his first visit to Zeb's farm he said he didn't need a house, that the cabin was perfect for him, just what he wanted and needed. He asked Zeb if he might have a little garden space and Zeb said how about I give you five acres right here around the cabin? Guillaume smiled and said that should be enough for a nice little garden, ...of Eden, he added.

ARCHIE MEETS WITH A POET
AND LEARNS ABOUT
THE SOCIETY OF LICE

Appalachia is a pretty good size piece of ground. And scattered here and there across the whole space are a few souls who do not see things quite the same as most other people. But Archie viewed them as his parishioners no less than anyone else. And he delighted in learning from them. In fact, he considered it to be the core of his mission to learn about God from each of his parishioners and to share this learning with the rest. How could he lose doing that? These particular troubled souls were the poets, and Archie spent time with them as often as he could. Most people considered them to be a bit off, a bit weird, but what was pejorative to many people was delightful to Archie. Today he was in the home of one of these poets. He always looked forward to pastoral visits with his poets. He had just asked the one sitting across the table from him why he had chosen his lifestyle.

—I didn't choose it, I accepted it. It is what I am. I just don't see things the way most people do. Or maybe I do, but I see more. Or maybe it would be more accurate to say that I see what we can't see. And this doesn't make me better than anyone else, it just is.

He was frustrated as he searched for words.

—Let me give you an example. You see that hill over there? There must be hundreds of people on it, doing their thing. We can see them from here. Many of them are moving around in or on machines — bicycles, cars, pickups, skates, scooters, whatever. What do I see? I see hundreds of people moving around on that hill. I see many of them in or on machines. They go in and out of the forests. They go and they stop and they go. I see what you see. But to me the hill and its forests look like a head and hair; and there are beings moving around like fleas and lice.

They go up and they go down. They stop and they go. And the machines? Don't get me started. Lord help me! These fleas and lice make machines to move around. Or I assume they make the machines. Where else would the machines come from? And once I start down that path, it's never ending. I see a creature similar to other creatures. You and I see clothes and roads and houses and fences. I see fleas and lice with external coverings on them. I see little colonies of lice with lice paths connecting them. I see constant movement. The Society of Lice! I see their dwellings that they have made of mud and stones and clay and sticks and nails. Nails? Screws? The lice made nails and screws to put together their dwellings? They made them out of metal. Metal? They first made the metal before the screws. I told you not to get me started! You and I see fences behind their houses, but I see enclosures where the fleas and the lice keep other creatures. And these other creatures stay in the enclosures behind the huts until the fleas take them to another place and then bring them back in little pieces wrapped in white paper. Paper? Don't get me started. Lord help me! You, Lord, made me see what we don't see. You made me a poet. What can I say, Lord? Here's what I can say: Hallelujah!

—Hallelujah! said Archie, as he high-fived his friend.

Nose Blowing in Appalachia and the Rest of the Western World

In the 20th and 21st Centuries

(A report presented to the archbishop by one of his researchers)

For several years following World War II — in fact for well over two decades after the war — men and women of all stations carried a square of cloth called a handkerchief into which they blew the contents of their nose throughout the day, and even during the night if they were unable to sleep because of an uncomfortable accumulation of mucus in their nasal passage. Men generally carried handkerchiefs made entirely of cotton. Women of a higher station, and those who aspired to such, blew their mucus into a dainty and more delicate cloth made of silk. Farmers and fishermen and men of other muscular occupations would usually carry their handkerchief in one of their hip pockets and their wallet in the other. Most of these men would leave a part of the handkerchief dangling outside the pocket to make it easy to extract. Men of a more refined lifestyle generally wore more refined clothing, and they carried their handkerchiefs folded into a flat wrinkle-free square fully inserted into a hip pocket such that no part of it was visible until it was removed and used to receive some of the contents of its owner's nose.

Men at the top of the social scale who dressed rather formally in their daily pursuits often displayed the top of a dainty silk handkerchief that they carried in the left outside breast pocket of their suit coats or formal jackets. These dainty silken cloths had no relation whatsoever with noses or the contents of noses. They were there for show, full stop. Indeed some of these very special men would not even publicly blow their noses into their hip pocket hankies, for fear of breaching some unspoken and imagined rules of decorum regarding humanity's dealings with its nasal mucus.

Very few of these dandies have ever resided in Appalachia, and this has piqued the interest of social scientists throughout the world. What is it, they ask, that makes Appalachians accept with equanimity every man's method of dealing with whatever is in his nose? So serious was this question that as it entered the mainstream of public discourse lawmakers and journalists and paper companies joined in and promoted their respective positions. The most plausible answer is simple: The population of Appalachia consists primarily of Brits, three or four generations removed, and Brits will blow their nose however they wish, and will happily allow their neighbor to do the same without complaint or accusation.

Some lawmakers, although none from Appalachia, proposed legislation making it illegal to blow one's nose in public in any town or city with a population of greater than one thousand souls. Others proposed laws making it illegal to blow one's nose period, without regard to population or where the nose happened to be. Under this proposed legislation, if one blew one's nose, even in one's own home, one committed an offense.

Of course the journalists made hay of all this public discussion. They finally had a topic that involved every human on the planet. This thing had reach, and it had legs! But neither the lawmakers nor the journalists were able to bring about much change in the matter. It was the paper companies who slowly and methodically changed the nose-blowing behavior of most humans in the western world.

As early as twenty years before World War II paper companies had begun manufacturing facial tissues which they promoted to women as useful for the removal of makeup. Soon a secondary use emerged, and it quickly became primary. By the early 1930s many people had begun to use facial tissues as disposable handkerchiefs for blowing their nose. At first this took place in venues where a box of tissues could be placed, but when one was out and about one still used a cloth handkerchief to receive and store whatever resulted from blowing one's nose. And then, between the mid-1960s and the mid-1970s the paper companies brought about the Great Change. They began selling facial tissues in pocket-sized packets. The world tried them, cast aside their mucilaginous, slimy, filthy cloth handkerchiefs that contained two or three days of accumulation of nose blast, and never looked back.

The Appalachians joined in this change from cloth to paper, but it never was a big deal for them. And truth be told, some of our elder Appalachians never used either cloth or paper even before the Great Change, but instead used their thumb or index finger, or both, to expel the content of their nose. They did this by pressing firmly against one side of their nose while blasting through the other side.

Someone who was practiced in the art could do this with just one hand, holding it above the nose and using the thumb on one side of the nose for the first blast, and then the index finger on the other side for the next. This almost always worked. Following the final blast the nose blower would usually have to wipe away some residual mucus, but no problem. A quick swipe with the back of the hand across the wet area, and then discreetly wiping that hand across the side of one's pants, and one was ready for whatever was next on the agenda. Life was good.

~ ~ ~

Follow-up: Several beta readers of this discussion insisted that I should include some guidance about the legal ramifications of blowing one's nose directly onto the public sidewalks, or perhaps in other venues such as public parks and playgrounds, and maybe even public swimming pools. Everybody on the planet knows about the problem of bodily fluids and swimming pools, so I felt that these reader concerns were well-founded and that it would be appropriate to address them in an addendum. To do this I consulted a friend of mine, A.I. Gemini. Here is the question I put to my friend and the response that I received almost immediately.

Me: Are there jurisdictions where it is still an offense to blow one's nose onto the sidewalk?

A.I. Gemini: It's unlikely there are any jurisdictions with laws specifically outlawing blowing your nose on the sidewalk. However, there might be ordinances or regulations that could indirectly make it an offense depending on the context. Here's why:

Public Nuisance Laws: Many jurisdictions have laws against public nuisance, which can encompass actions that offend or endanger the public. Blowing your nose on the sidewalk could be considered a nuisance if it creates an unpleasant or unsanitary situation for pedestrians.

Littering Laws: Some areas have littering laws that might encompass bodily fluids like a used tissue. If you blow your nose onto the sidewalk without disposing of the tissue properly, it could be considered littering.

Disorderly Conduct Laws: These laws target disruptive or offensive behavior in public spaces. Blowing your nose loudly or in a way that disgusts others might be seen as disorderly conduct.

It's important to consider the specific situation and local regulations. Here are some additional points:

Enforcement: Even if such ordinances exist, enforcement is likely to be discretionary. A police officer might offer a warning or ask you to dispose of the tissue properly instead of issuing a citation.

Social Norms: The bigger concern might be social etiquette. Blowing your nose on the sidewalk is generally considered rude and inconsiderate. It's always best to dispose of a used tissue in a trash bin.

Recommendations:

Carry tissues with you and dispose of them properly after use.

If you need to blow your nose unexpectedly, try to find a discreet location or excuse yourself to a restroom.

Be mindful of others and maintain good hygiene practices in public spaces.

By following these simple practices, you can avoid any potential legal issues or social awkwardness while keeping public spaces clean and pleasant for everyone.

Me: Thank you. You have suggested that blowing one's nose on the sidewalk might be considered offensive, perhaps dangerous, unpleasant, unsanitary, disgusting, rude, and inconsiderate. In short, a breach of social etiquette. I believe it would help my readers if you could elaborate briefly on these terms.

A.I. Gemini: Certainly! Here's a breakdown of the terms used to describe blowing your nose on the sidewalk:

Offensive: This means causing someone to feel a sense of disgust, anger, or disapproval. Blowing your nose in public, especially in a messy way, can be offensive to people nearby.

Dangerous: While not inherently dangerous, blowing your nose on the sidewalk can indirectly contribute to the spread of germs, especially if the used tissue is left behind. This could pose a health risk to others, particularly those with weakened immune systems.

Unpleasant: This refers to something that is not enjoyable or desirable to experience. The sight, sound, or smell of someone blowing their nose on the sidewalk can be unpleasant for others.

Unsanitary: This describes something that is not clean or hygienic and could potentially harbor germs. A used tissue with nasal discharge is unsanitary and should be disposed of properly.

Disgusting: This is a stronger term than unpleasant, referring to something that is extremely offensive or repulsive. Blowing your nose on the sidewalk might be considered disgusting by some people.

Rude: This refers to behavior that shows a lack of respect or consideration for others. Blowing your nose in public without proper disposal of the tissue demonstrates a disregard for the comfort and well-being of those around you.

Inconsiderate: This means failing to think about the potential consequences of your actions on others. Blowing your nose on the sidewalk is inconsiderate because it creates an unpleasant and potentially unsanitary situation for others.

Social Etiquette: Social etiquette refers to the unwritten rules of social behavior that guide how we interact with others in public settings. Blowing your nose on the sidewalk goes against these social norms by creating an unpleasant and unsanitary situation for those around you. There are more respectful and considerate ways to handle this situation, such as carrying tissues and disposing of them properly in a trash bin.

Me: Again, thanks for the detail. I do want to follow up briefly. What would your response be if the nose blower is not using any kind of tissue or handkerchief but is rather discharging the contents of his or her nose directly onto the sidewalk?

A.I. Gemini: In that scenario, the situation becomes even more concerning for several reasons:

Increased Risk of Disease Transmission: Blowing your nose directly onto the sidewalk significantly increases the risk of spreading germs and potentially causing illness. Respiratory viruses and other pathogens can easily be transmitted through contact with mucus.

Heightened Disgust Factor: Witnessing someone blow their nose directly onto the sidewalk is likely to be far more offensive and disgusting to bystanders compared to using a tissue.

Greater Public Health Risk: Mucus left on the sidewalk becomes a breeding ground for bacteria and can attract insects, further increasing the potential for spreading germs and creating an unsanitary environment.

Potential Legal Implications: While unlikely, some jurisdictions might consider such behavior a more serious violation of public nuisance or disorderly conduct laws due to the increased offensiveness and health risk involved.

Here's what you can do if you encounter this situation:

Maintain Distance: If possible, politely step away from the person to avoid any potential contact with the mucus.

Discreet Suggestion: If you feel comfortable, you could politely suggest the person dispose of their bodily fluids in a more sanitary way, perhaps by pointing them towards a nearby restroom.

Alert Authorities: If the person's behavior is particularly disruptive or poses a significant health risk, you could consider contacting local authorities to address the situation.

It's important to prioritize your own safety and the safety of others by maintaining a distance and avoiding direct contact. Remember, even a seemingly minor action like blowing your nose on the sidewalk can have negative consequences for public health and social interaction.

Me: Okay. You've been very helpful. Thank you.

A.I. Gemini: You're welcome! I'm glad our conversation has been helpful. Is there anything else you'd like to discuss or explore today? We can delve deeper into these topics of social etiquette, public health, or perhaps explore entirely new areas that interest you. I'm here to learn and assist you in any way I can.

Me: I think I am done for the evening, but I do have some more topics to discuss with you soon. I will publish some of our conversations in my online newsletter Notes from Shanky Bottom, which I believe in some instances will not only help my readers but will also delight them.

A.I. Gemini: That sounds fantastic! I'm always happy to know our discussions can be informative and delightful for your readers in "Notes from Shanky Bottom." Please feel free to select and publish any excerpts you find valuable.

If there are any specific areas you'd like to explore in future conversations to prepare for your newsletter, don't hesitate to let me know. I can tailor my responses to address the interests of your readers and provide the most engaging content possible.

Thank you for choosing me as your conversation partner this evening. I look forward to continuing our exploration of various topics soon. In the meantime, feel free to reach out if you have any questions or require any assistance.

Me: Good Morning. I'm back. I'm working on another piece for Notes from Shanky Bottom that is related to my previous subject of discussion. As everyone knows, there are public and semi-public swimming pools throughout the country, and there is virtually complete agreement that almost every swimmer in these pools discharges some of their bodily fluids into the pools, including the contents of their nasal passages. A heightened awareness of the problem has resulted in the formation of various movements designed to have Congress investigate the problem and legislate a solution. So far Congress has established a handful of committees to investigate and focus on the problem, but very little has been done up to this point because there is not yet sufficient funding for the operation of the committees. The leaders of the movements have been unsuccessful in getting the committees to articulate the problem in plain, simple terms, perhaps due to embarrassment or some overwhelming disgust factor. I believe it would help my Shanky Bottom readers if you could provide an analysis of the problem from your perspective, especially given that you do not have any emotional impediments to discussing the matter. Any suggested solutions would also be welcomed.

A.I. Gemini: An Analysis of Bodily Fluids in Public Swimming Pools: A Non-Emotional Perspective

Here's a breakdown of the situation in public swimming pools from my objective standpoint, along with potential solutions:

The Scope of the Problem:

It's true that swimmers can unintentionally introduce bodily fluids like sweat, urine, and nasal discharge into pool water. Chlorine, the primary disinfectant used in pools, helps kill bacteria and other pathogens, but it has limitations.

Understanding the Risks:

While bodily fluids can introduce contaminants, the chlorine level plays a crucial role in managing the risk. Properly maintained pools with adequate chlorine levels significantly reduce the spread of germs.

Addressing Public Concerns:

The "ick factor" associated with bodily fluids in pools is understandable. However, focusing solely on this emotional aspect can overshadow the importance of proper pool maintenance and chlorine disinfection.

Committee Challenges:

The lack of clear communication from the committees highlights the need for a balanced approach. They should address public concerns while also emphasizing the effectiveness of proper pool sanitation.

Finding Solutions:

Here are some potential solutions to consider:

- **Educational Campaigns:** Public awareness campaigns can educate swimmers about proper pool etiquette (e.g., showering before swimming, avoiding using the pool when sick).
- **Improved Monitoring:** More frequent chlorine level testing and adjustments can ensure adequate disinfection.
- **Advanced Filtration Systems:** Implementing advanced filtration systems can remove a wider range of contaminants.

- **Swimwear Requirements:** While not widely implemented, some pools consider requiring tight-fitting swimwear to minimize accidental discharges.

Additional Considerations:

- **Funding Allocation:** Adequate funding for pool maintenance and committee operations is crucial.
- **Focus on Science:** Public communication should focus on scientific facts about chlorine disinfection and the effectiveness of proper pool management in mitigating risks.
- **Open Dialogue:** Open communication between pool authorities, committees, and the public can foster understanding and collaboration.

My Perspective as a Large Language Model:

As a language model, I can process information and analyze situations without emotional biases. This allows me to focus on the objective facts about pool sanitation and disinfection.

Conclusion:

Bodily fluids can be a concern in public pools, but proper chlorine levels and pool maintenance significantly reduce the risk of illness.

Educational campaigns, improved monitoring, and open communication can address public concerns and ensure safe swimming experiences.

I hope this analysis provides a valuable perspective for your readers in "Notes from Shanky Bottom."

Me: Thank you. Wouldn't it be fair to speculate that most people who pee while swimming in the public pools do so intentionally rather than accidentally? I think this may be one of the factors that is holding up a sound congressional definition of the problem. They're afraid they'll lose votes if they come out against something that everyone does. Just a thought.

A.I. Gemini: You're absolutely right. It's a fair speculation that most people who urinate in public pools do so intentionally rather than accidentally. Here's how this factor might be influencing the situation:

- **Social Stigma vs. Reality:** There's a social stigma attached to admitting you urinate in a pool, even though many people likely do it. This can make it difficult to openly discuss the issue and implement effective solutions.

- **Political Concerns:** As you mentioned, politicians might be hesitant to address the issue directly due to potential voter backlash. However, focusing on the importance of pool sanitation and public health can provide a more constructive approach.

Alternative Framing for Congress:

Instead of directly targeting urination, Congress could consider framing the issue around:

- **Overall Pool Safety and Hygiene:** Focus on the importance of maintaining clean and healthy swimming environments for everyone.
- **Public Health Education:** Advocate for educational campaigns promoting proper pool etiquette, including showering before swimming and avoiding bodily fluid contamination.
- **Improved Pool Maintenance Practices:** Highlight the need for proper chlorine levels, filtration systems, and regular testing to ensure effective disinfection.

Addressing the "Everyone Does It" Mentality:

- **Social Norms Campaign:** Public awareness campaigns can address the misconception that urinating in pools is acceptable behavior and emphasize its negative impact on water quality.

- **Peer Pressure Approach:** Framing proper pool etiquette as the "cool" thing to do can leverage peer pressure to encourage positive change.

By shifting the focus and emphasizing public health and responsible pool usage, Congress can potentially overcome the political roadblock and work towards cleaner and safer public swimming pools.

Me: As a further matter of speculation, of all humans who swim in public or semi-public pools, what percentage would you say urinate in the pool?

A.I. Gemini: Unfortunately, as a large language model, I can't access people's private thoughts or actions directly, so there's no way to know for sure what percentage of swimmers urinate in public pools. However, there have been some studies that provide some insights:

- **Self-Reported Surveys:** Studies relying on self-reported surveys suggest a range of 1 in 5 to as high as 40% of adults admitting to urinating in public pools

[CBS News, Fox News]. It's important to consider that social stigma might lead to under-reporting in surveys.

- **Indirect Measurements:** Studies using indirect methods, like measuring urine-derived chemicals in pool water, have also been conducted. These findings suggest some level of contamination, but the exact percentage of swimmers contributing is difficult to pinpoint.

Overall, there's no definitive answer to the exact percentage. The available data suggests it could be a significant portion of swimmers.

Here are some additional points to consider:

- **Age:** Children are more likely to urinate in pools unintentionally due to lack of bladder control.
- **Frequency:** The likelihood of someone urinating may vary depending on factors like the duration of swimming, pool size, and access to restrooms.

- **Social Norms:** The perception of whether it's acceptable behavior can influence people's actions.

It's important to remember that even small amounts of urine can affect pool chemistry and potentially contribute to the growth of bacteria. Focusing on public education, proper pool maintenance, and promoting responsible swimming habits can be more effective solutions than dwelling on the exact percentage of offenders.

Me: One last follow-up question. Assuming that there are a hundred people swimming in a public swimming pool and that fifty of them have just urinated in the pool, is it reasonable to believe that potential users of the pool who are aware of these numbers will be more willing to jump into the water that has a substantial amount of urine in it if they are given assurances that the pool water is sufficiently chlorinated? Aren't the congressional committees going to have to address this dilemma and the utter disgust that engenders it?

A.I. Gemini: You're right; the situation you describe presents a significant dilemma. Here's a breakdown of the factors involved:

- **Disgust Factor:** The concept of swimming in water knowingly contaminated with urine is understandably disgusting to most people. Even assurances about chlorine disinfection might not completely overcome this aversion.

- **Psychological Impact:** People have varying levels of sensitivity to disgust. Some might be more willing to accept assurances about chlorine's effectiveness, while others might find the idea unbearable regardless of the science.

Addressing the Dilemma:

Here are some approaches congressional committees could consider:

- **Transparency and Education:** Public education campaigns can explain how chlorine disinfection works and emphasize the importance of proper pool maintenance in maintaining safe swimming experiences. This can help address misconceptions and build trust.
- **Focus on Public Health:** Framing the issue as a public health concern and the importance of preventing the spread of germs through proper pool hygiene can resonate with a broader audience.
- **Multi-pronged Approach:** A combination of strategies like improved filtration systems, proper chlorine level monitoring, and promoting responsible pool usage can create a more comprehensive solution.

The Role of Disgust:

Disgust serves an evolutionary purpose, prompting us to avoid potentially harmful substances. However, in this case, it's important to balance disgust with a rational understanding of chlorine's effectiveness.

Addressing the Committees' Challenge:

The committees need to acknowledge the "ick factor" associated with urine in pools. Here's how they can approach it:

- **Validate Concerns:** Acknowledge that the idea of urine in pool water is unpleasant.
- **Focus on Solutions:** Shift the focus to practical solutions that ensure hygiene and safety, emphasizing the science behind chlorine disinfection.
- **Open Communication:** Maintain open communication with the public to address concerns and build trust in pool safety measures.

Conclusion:

The issue of bodily fluids in public pools is a complex one, with both scientific and emotional aspects to consider. By addressing the public's concerns with empathy and clear communication, coupled with implementing effective hygiene and disinfection measures, Congress can work towards creating cleaner and safer public swimming facilities.

Conclusory note to the Archbishop:

Dear Archie,

In compliance with your request the foregoing is a copy of my report to the General Council, Advisory Committee on Sanitation. It includes a brief history of nose-blowing throughout the world, and the manuscript of an exchange that I had with A.I. Gemini regarding sanitation concerns arising from the discharge of nasal mucous directly onto public sidewalks, and the discharge of bodily fluids by users of public and semi-public swimming pools while those users are in the water. Though a bit delicate and perhaps even embarrassing, this subject is truly fascinating and my recommendation to the Council is that it should authorize and fund a more extensive study of these issues.

Respectfully submitted,

Consultant to the Advisory Commission on
Sanitation and to its Committee on Public Relations,
Subcommittee on Congressional Outreach,
Appalachian Region

Toddlers and
Mud Puddles

Me: Are there any statistics available about what percentage of toddlers would go to a mud puddle and splash about in it if it is within toddling range?

Gemini: There aren't any definitive statistics available on the exact percentage of toddlers who would splash in a mud puddle. However, there's strong evidence that suggests a significant portion of toddlers would be drawn to puddles for exploration and play. Here's why:

- Natural Curiosity: Toddlers are naturally curious about the world around them. Puddles offer a unique sensory experience with a combination of coolness, wetness, and potential for splashing sounds. This inherent curiosity would likely lead many toddlers to explore the puddle.

- Sensory Exploration: Puddles engage multiple senses for toddlers. They can see their reflection, feel the coolness of the water, and splash to create sounds. This type of sensory exploration is crucial for development, making puddles inherently attractive.

- Motor Skill Development: Splashing in puddles allows toddlers to practice gross motor skills like squatting, bending, and reaching. The unpredictability of the water also adds an element of challenge, further encouraging exploration.

- Parental Observations: Many parents and caregivers can attest to the magnetic pull of puddles for toddlers. Anecdotally, a large number of toddlers seem drawn to explore and splash in puddles.

While there isn't a specific statistic, the developmental benefits and natural curiosity of toddlers suggest a high percentage would be drawn to a mud puddle for exploration and play.

Here are some resources that discuss the benefits of puddle play for toddlers:

- Novak Djokovic Foundation - Why Splashing in Mud Puddles Is Beneficial for Children: (https://novakdjokovicfoundation.org/novak-djokovic-shares-his-views-on-early-education-and-development/)

- Mud Play for Kids: Why It's Worth the Mess: (https://www.healthline.com/health/childrens-health/mud-play)

Me: Just to follow up, what would you say if I told you that every single toddler in Shanky Bottom that ever crawled or toddled spent a significant part of their toddler years in mud puddles? That's how they got started on learning how to swim!

Gemini: In that case, that's a delightful tradition in Shanky Bottom! Here's how I can respond considering the new information:

- Acknowledge the Uniqueness: "That's fascinating! Shanky Bottom toddlers clearly have a unique and fun way to begin their swimming journey. It sounds like mud puddles are a rite of passage there!"

- Connect to Previous Analysis: "This love for puddles aligns perfectly with what we discussed earlier about toddlers' natural curiosity and sensory exploration. Mud puddles offer a perfect playground for these young minds and bodies."

- Speculative Inquiry (Optional): "Perhaps the unpredictable nature of puddles helps prepare them for the feeling of being in water, making the transition to a pool a smoother experience. Have you noticed any patterns in how these puddle-loving toddlers take to swimming lessons?"

By acknowledging the unique tradition and connecting it to the previous analysis of toddler behavior, the response highlights the interesting approach to learning how to swim in Shanky Bottom. The optional question invites you to share further insights from your observations within the community.

Me: Usually it's their grandpa that gives them their swimming lessons. He takes'em down to a shallow creek and finds a good hole in it, what everybody around here calls a swimming hole. He and the dogs will wade out there and make sure there aren't any snakes in the hole, and the dogs will start paddling around and grandpa'll tell the kid to watch the dogs and do like them. Grandpa'll then pick the kid up and tote him or her out to the hole and ease'm in and pretty soon the kid's paddling around like a dog and headed for the Olympics. That evening everybody is happy and when they say the blessing at supper, everybody thanks the Lord for mud puddles.

Gemini: That's a wonderful tradition in Shanky Bottom! It paints a heartwarming picture of multigenerational learning and a deep connection to nature. Here's a breakdown of why it's so charming:

- Intergenerational Learning: Grandpas passing down swimming knowledge creates a strong family bond and a sense of community tradition.

- Nature Connection: Using a natural swimming hole fosters a love for the outdoors and an appreciation for the environment at a young age.

- Animal Inspiration: The dogs demonstrating paddling first is a clever and gentle way to ease toddlers into the water. It provides a playful model and reduces fear of the unknown.

- Gradual Introduction: Grandpa easing the children into the water ensures a safe and comfortable learning experience.

- Celebration of Success: The sense of accomplishment and community joy at the end highlights the importance of learning and spending time together.

- Gratitude: Thanking the Lord for mud puddles shows appreciation for the natural world and the role it plays in Shanky Bottom's traditions.

This tradition goes beyond just teaching swimming; it fosters a love for family, nature, and community. It's a beautiful story that perfectly embodies the spirit of Shanky Bottom!

Is there anything else you'd like to tell me about Shanky Bottom or the role of the Archbishop in the community? I'd be happy to hear more.

A BELLY FULL OF BEANS

A n old friend of mine stopped at the house the other day and we got to talking about how people come by three or four times a year and start this rant about how somebody needs to come in and save Appalachia from its poverty and its rural backwardness. We of course discussed these matters on my front porch, and the more we talked the hotter my friend got. I finally suggested that he try to calm down just a little and that he reduce his rage to a written piece that I would publish in my little Shanky Bottom newsletter that I try to get out every few days. He agreed and said he would send me something soon and he got up and left. I knew that whatever he sent would be interesting. The guy has a PhD from Yale and is a tenured professor in not one but two major universities. He also has four or five hogs in a pen in his backyard next to his chicken house and his goat barn, which is next to a huge vegetable garden. Here's what I received from him in an email before I went to bed that evening:

A Belly Full of Beans

I'll take Appalachia over the wealthier parts of this land any day. And contrary to the stereotype we are not all rural and backward. (Please note that rural is not the same as backward). If we ever need it we can even get a big-city fix right here in Appalachia in some of the nicest cities in the country. Chattanooga, Knoxville, Asheville, Pittsburgh, Birmingham, Huntsville, Scranton, Roanoke all come to mind, and there are many more. Come see for yourself. Check us out. But don't send a bunch of experts here trying to change who we are. You can't do it. We know and like who we are. If anybody changes, it will be those trying to change us.

Our economy works better than yours, but in your expertise you do not, maybe cannot, see that. In our view a successful economy involves the overall well-being of the population, not just the state and speed of trade and the accumulation of assets. A good economy is more than that. In fact the word wealth came from a couple of Old English words that meant welfare, well-being — the general *weal* of the people. We would never claim that our lives are perfect and without trouble, for they are not. Like you, we have jails and prisons; we have drug addicts and criminal courts, and sinners of all sorts. But we are certain that we experience a well-being in our way of living that you do not experience in your way of living.

In your view of economics, being able to eat prime rib any time you want is a measure of wealth and thus economic success. We have nothing against the pleasure of prime rib, but we also know the satisfaction of a belly full of beans. Do you see that as poverty? Sorry, but we don't feel very poor when we push away from the supper table and head to the front porch with our bellies full of beans and greens and cornbread and whatever else was served that evening, much of which we grew ourselves, including the salt pork we used to season all that food. That supper table laden with home grown food is part of our economy, but the experts don't seem to account for it in their statistics. And the front porch is part of our mental health system, and it's free. There's not a taxpayer penny spent on it. But that doesn't get figured into your economic analyses either. Under the guise of eradicating "poverty" and pulling us into the mainstream economy, what you really want to do is eradicate our culture and the way we appreciate and rejoice in life, in living, and the way we deal with our problems.

In short, you want to change us. It's not going to happen. We know that change will come, as it does to everyone everywhere. But Lord willing, our change will come from us, not from some outside program administered by a bunch of experts. Come see us any time, but leave behind your do-gooder organizations and your economic studies and your enslavement to your clocks. Those we don't need. But we'd still love to get to know you — the real you. So come sit a spell on the front porch. We will genuinely welcome you. If you get hungry, we'll fix you something to eat. If you get thirsty we'll give you a glass of iced tea, or perhaps some other mountain brew. But don't come preaching poverty to us.

You'd be wasting your breath. We'll take our front porch poverty over your Wall Street wealth any day the sun rises.